Contents....

Life And Honour

Mathew had slogged ten years for this moment. It had been a tough haul, but it was worth it. He had come to Mumbai, to complete his Masters in Commerce and had then stayed on, succumbing to the lure of its hues and avenues. Mumbai tended to grow on you, especially when you had migrated from a one bullock cart township on the outskirts of Madurai. The bullock cart part was not strictly true. There was a lot of money in these small-time towns, although one was never really sure where the money came from and where it went. Attitudes were still parochial and intellectual pursuits confined to the four well-guarded walls of the temple which still kept out the non-Brahmins. Mathew's father had been a professed agnostic. Mathews was a little ashamed of the fact that his father had converted to Christendom to gain favour with his mother, a staff nurse at the mission hospital. It was she who had got him the admissions in Mumbai, through her uncle, who was the Parish priest in the Dominique's church. Christian credentials and the priestly influence of

his uncle secured him a hostel accommodation in the YMCA.

The stay at the YMCA had moulded him and made him who he was. There were a lot of hard-working young men staying in the same dorms. They were all from disparate backgrounds, yet driven by the shared desire to succeed and to do good. This amalgam of success and goodness was probably misplaced idealism in Mumbai, where young men and women were easily lured by easy money and short cuts to windfalls and constantly waltzed and teetered on the brink of legality. They were all idealists in a way. They did not consider money or success as an end but as a route to influence they could exert for the common good of humanity. There were a few bad apples in the packet. They lived their own lives, dabbling in drugs and depravity, but they kept to themselves and did not interfere with the group Mathew was in.

He had finished his Master's with honours and was eager to go back to his roots, but it was not to be. He had gone around with his father, to the local Barons of influence and trade and had been scorned and ridiculed. There was no one interested in a Bombay trained youth with aspirations. Most businesses were family concerns and outsiders were considered menial employees. Both he and his father had been relieved when a multinational bank selected him on probation. The competition had been tough and the selection processes steep. But Mathews had survived. There is little that can stop a hard-working man whose capabilities and diligence matched his ambition. Mathews' rise through the ranks was unspectacular but steady.

The promotion to Vice President had placed him in a different league altogether. Multinational companies were as hierarchical as governmental organizations. Here the power was more real. The youngsters now looked to him for inspiration, copying his moves and keen to make an impression on a rising star. The Bank also accepted him into their inner circle. He was now one of them, his fate tied with that of the organization and they looked after him well. Consider the new flat he had been allotted. It was on the 10th floor, overlooking the national stadium. This was a stadium where cricket test matches were played and major concerts held. He would have gallery seats now on, and watch the proceeds from the comfort of his house.

Ayesha, his wife had been ecstatic on seeing their flat. Split level three-bedroom houses in the city were only for the cream of society. There were a few of apartments in the complex owned by movie stars and cricket icons. A large number seemed to belong to politicians of various hues. Their bank had a few flats on lease from a fictitious owner who was a front for a serving cabinet minister. The Mathew's thought Ayesha, had arrived on the social scene. The euphoria did not last long. The bank he worked for was embroiled in a financial scandal on the wrong side of the political divide. The Mumbai office closed. Mathews had to find another job in an Indian Bank and move to another less elegant flat.

They had been married for five years now. And for the past five years Ayesha had been chronically unhappy. Ayesha's fascination with her husband had waned from the time of her honeymoon. He was, as she explained to her friends and to her parents, a looser in every way. Physically he was unimpressive in every way. He did not dress well and he did not have the suave sophistication of the successful young men she had encountered every day in the corporate world. Mathews had been disheartened by her rejection, but it had worked for him. The disgust with which she viewed him and her persistent disdain was a constant deterrent against complacency.

Ayesha's father was a senior executive in the railways. With indulgent parents and the army of personnel at their disposal she had a pampered childhood. The Indian Railways is the largest employer in the country and there were hordes of helpers to take her to school, to arts class or the swimming pool. Shifting out with Mathews had been a big letdown. If there had been something about him that she could admire, or if he had been a great lover or a stimulating conversationalist, maybe she could have tolerated him. He was none of that and to make matters worse he had to spent long hours in his office.

It had been difficult for Ayesha to reconcile to the life style a middle level executive could offer. Mathews was never at home. Their old apartment was in one of the many structures in Mumbai which seemed to be in imminent danger of falling down. The neighbours were all middle-class employees in various government jobs. Each flat was packed with three and in some cases four generations, competing for space and dominance. There was constant bickering about the water supply and as to who should use the lifts. Their house had been quite small and the plaster kept peeling off the walls. Ayesha had to constantly make excuses to her friends who wanted to come over and visit. After a while they stopped asking. Ayesha had the sinking sensation that she was stuck with a looser. It was only her pride which prevented her from going back to her father's place.

General elections to parliament upended fortunes again. Mathews old bank was on favourable terms with the new party in power. Mumbai operations of the bank started again. Many of the senior managers had moved on to other multinationals. They would not return. Mathews was reinstated. Mathews persistent performance, though unspectacular made the management comfortable. He was reinstated. An upmarket apartment was allotted to him. He was vice president again and part of the inner circle. The rags to riches swing unsettled Mathews. Ayesha took it in her stride.

Overnight things changed. Ayesha had spent a mini-fortune to do up their new flat. For the first time in her life she could contemplate continuing her marriage without a divorce. Divorces were messy affairs. Why would anyone want to launder their dirty linen in public? Ayesha had always felt that a marriage should be a limited period contract. You renewed the contract every few years if you were so inclined. Else you moved on with your life. Today, a marriage was like a life sentence. With a time limited contract, if you did not like your partner, you could just walk away. It was expected of many unhappy women to suffer an eternity of discomfiture and a lifetime of painful reconciliation to fate.

Mathews had been a little concerned at the amount of money Ayesha was spending on the apartment. He had always been a bit of a scrooge. The company had paid a part of the experiences for renovation of a flat which was already pretty spectacular. The rest of the money was Ayesha's own. They had a minor argument over the extent of work to be done. Mathews' attitude had only served to heighten her disdain of him. This was the basic point of discord. He was only too eager to settle into domestic complacency. She wanted to keep her options open. An open ended limited tenure marriage would have been excellent. Ayesha would definitely have moved on. In fact, most of the people she knew would have benefited from an open marriage, thought Ayesha. For one thing, it would keep people more competitive and agile. Marriage was a relic of an era when women were dependent on men and traded their bodies for security. Ayesha had always been careful about her figure. She was an artist and was intensely aware of her own and others' imperfections. She spent the whole day painting. It did not get her much money. She however was quite passionate about her art and was confident that, given the right breaks she could break into the big league.

One room in the new apartment had been modified into a mini art gallery. This was a largish room and the walls were full of her paintings. She painted the human form. Walking along the road, she would see a rickshaw driver or a beggar and create an abstract image of the man or woman on canvas. Ayesha had put a mattress on the floor, where she could relax to rejuvenate her artistic exuberance. There were mirrors along the walls and on the ceiling. Lying on the mattress she could see herself amongst her paintings. There was a small refrigerator in the corner she had stocked up with juices and snacks and a few cans of beer. There were canvasses all over in various stages of completion. Ayesha believed in starting a series of projects at the same time. Occasionally, she would get inspired and stay on at a canvass for days till the painting was finished. Till then she would shift from canvas to canvas, adding a few strokes to each every day. Occasionally she would get a model home and spend a few hours with them in her room, while she captured the essence of their being in paints and pastels.

Mathews remembered the time he first met her. His boss had asked him to pick up some contemporary art to gift an important overseas customer. It was Mathew's first visit to the art gallery. He had no idea about paintings or their value. He looked around helplessly. His manager had been quite curt and unhelpful. There was no time for him to do any research. The customer would be in the boss's office in an hour. It was then that he saw this strikingly tall girl in faded jeans, who was making pencil sketches of some of the works. Mathew guessed that she would be an art student. He decided to ask her for help.

In normal circumstances Ayesha would have brushed off the young man's plea. It was an old pick-up line. "Can you help me choose a painting?" She had fallen for it once and had no intention of doing so again, although she had to concede that the fallout and follow through of the first episode had been quite enjoyable. But this young man's distress seemed genuine and Ayesha had some time to spare.

She had shown him around and helped him choose a small painting. He had mumbled his grateful thanks. As he was leaving, he had asked her for her telephone number. If the client was pleased with the gift, he would call up to thank her. Ayesha had obliged. The client loved the painting. Mathew's manager had complemented him on his taste in art. Ayesha had accepted Mathew's invitation to dinner. She had seemed a little peeved by his choice of restaurant, but they got along quite well. Mathew's obvious adoration flattered her. Soon they were seeing each regularly. In a month, they had got married.

Mathews was in the back seat of his company car. He tried to unwind by listening to some classical music. Traffic was irritatingly slow. It usually was at this time of the evening. Mathews usually avoided the peak hours. Most days, he worked late. After ten pm the roads were clear. Manoj, his driver would get him home in 30 minutes. The evening drive was terrible. It was seven now and he had been in the car already for over one hour. Outside, he could see the opera house. At this rate, he would be home only by eight. He had not told Ayesha that he would be home early. He wanted to surprise her and take her out to dinner at the new seven star hotel. Afterward they would go to the discotheque. They had a complementary membership of Twirl, the high end disco where the glitterati of Mumbai dropped by to unwind. The bank was one of the major financers of the venture and the vice presidents had some privileges.

Ayesha and he had gone for the opening ceremony of the hotel. It had been a star studded evening of lights and glitz. Ayesha had relished the exposure and experience. They had never found time to go there again. Today his firm was celebrating a merger with an overseas bank. His colleagues had gone out on a hired yatch for a wild night of partying at sea. These were wild affairs and with no danger of intrusive cops trying to muscle in for a bribe. The shirts came off as soon as they out of the harbour. Even in his bachelor days, he had not been comfortable at these dos. He found it remarkable that the same people who indulged in such wantonly undignified behaviour could function normally in office afterward without embarrassment.

A young lady driving a compact gave him a long look as they stopped at a signal. Success was indeed an aphrodisiac. Mathews was sure she would not have given him a second glance in the old days when he drove a battered old Maruti van to work. He sometimes wondered if Ayesha would treat him differently if they had met as strangers after he found success. She had been put off with him when he was struggling and that would always be her image of him. It was possible that her attitude would change over a period of time. He was still in love with her, but if she persisted with her thinly veiled contempt of him, it would be tragic.

Mathews was grateful to her. If it had not been for her, it was unlikely that he would have ever risen to the position of vice president. She was his lucky beacon. Tonight, they could go out for dinner and later to the discotheque. Ayesha would get to meet many of her friends from the arts world and she would be happy. Mathews had two left feet and despite a concerted effort at picking up some dance steps, he was uncomfortable on the floor. But with the lights and the music, it did not really matter. There were plenty of light-footed hunks, but not too many vice presidents of multinational firms around. He was sure that the manager would show them some deference and a bit of special treatment which would make Ayesha's day.

There were of course some successful men who were also physically graceful. Mathew sometimes wished that he was a good dancer like Paras, his neighbour. Paras was one of the playboys of the corporate world. He came from a business family. As a teenager Paras had wanted to be a movie star. He had the looks and his father had the contacts. His father was however averse to the idea of his already vagrant son loosing himself further in the light and glitz of the often shady entertainment world. Paras had been forced to attend business school at Australia by his authoritarian dad. When he came back his father had offered to finance any business venture he would choose.

Paras was enamoured with beautiful women. He had friends amongst the movie stars and the models. His proposal that he become a movie producer had been vetoed by his father. Father and son had come to a compromise. Paras now ran a premier advertising agency. He could remain in touch with his movie friends and nurture whatever little artistic traits he had. He loved his work and had hired a team of competent professionals. His business was successful. There was a constant stream of female visitors to his apartment. Paras had been coerced into marriage by his parents. His wife was a socialite who spent most of her time in Europe. She did not seem to mind his excesses as long as he let her live her life the way she wanted.

The driver was honking for the security man to open the gate. They had reached the apartment complex. Mathews closed the file he had been working on in the car. This was the advantage of having a chauffeur. You could relax in the back seat and sum up the office work before reaching home. He perched his spectacles at the tip of his nose and scanned through some reports. There were a few more things he could have tied up at the office before he left. The challenges were endless. But you had to take a break off and on. He closed his briefcase with look of determination. Security at the gate was excellent. There was electronic surveillance at the gate round the clock. The boom barrier opened only after he inserted his electronic identity card. Video cameras scanned them as they drove through to the basement car park to his allotted slot. The driver jumped out to hold the door open for him. He was holding his hand out offering to carry Mathew's briefcase up to the apartment. Mathew thanked him, but declined the offer. He was not yet snobbish enough to make his chauffer carry his brief case. The driver had pressed the lift button and the doors were now opening. He thanked the man and stepped in.

It was a very posh looking lift and had soft music playing round the clock. From its glass walls Mathew's watched the city roads recede beneath him as it rose up the walls of the magnificent building. Mathews was planning out the evening. Ayesha would be surprised. Tonight he would be charmer like Paras. He would pamper the day lights out of her. He took off his spectacles and placed them in a case in his pocket. The lift moved up fast and the door opened. He turned right to his apartment. He wished he had remembered to bring flowers. It really did not matter. There was diamond brooch at an outlet near Twirl that he would buy her. She had seen it on the night they had gone there, but he had been feeling a little broke at that time with all the renovation work at the apartment. There was a mischievous grin on his face as he plotted out the evening.

Suddenly Mathews froze. The front door of the apartment was opening. A handsome man, his white silk shirt partly open with lipstick marks on the collar and his shock of hair wantonly disarrayed was coming out. It was Paras. He seemed totally relaxed with the pleased smile on his face of a man who has just had a very good time. Behind Paras, Mathews caught a glimpse of a tall stately girl, who seemed naked under a transparent negligee walking back into the apartment. The girl had not seen him.

Ayesha! So this was it. Paras had scored again. He looked surprised on seeing Mathews at the door, but there was no consternation or panic. The man was superbly confident of himself. Paras smiled. It was a sneering condescending smile that made something snap in Mathew's head. The door had shut and they were alone on the landing.

Mathew launched himself at Paras in a blind fury, raining blows upon his face. Paras seemed totally taken aback. He had not expected this kind of a violent response. He stepped back with a shocked look on his face. His hand went up to his nose and came away wet with blood. He was a good three inches taller than Mathews and much fitter. With a sickening sensation Mathews realized that the advantage of surprise that he had was over. Paras would probably slaughter him. He wished Ayesha would come to the door and rescue him.

Mathews flinched at the look of fury on Paras' face. His face was flushed. He was breathing heavily and his nose was bleeding. Mathews took a step back. Paras had a determined look on his face as he stepped forward. This wimp had dared to hit him and break his handsome nose. He would teach him a lesson. He clenched his fist and lunged towards Mathews. Mathews had kept his briefcase down at the door preparing to ring the calling bell. Tripping over Mathew's briefcase, he lost his balance and lurched into Mathews, clutching at the railing for support. Mathews moved quickly. This was his chance. He had started the fight and now he could finish it. If he allowed Paras to recover, he would get slaughtered. Stepping nimbly to one side, he caught fold of Paras' shirt and with one push – toppled him over the railing. Paras grunted as he tried to catch the railing. He could not hold on. There was a series of thuds as Paras bounced from wall to wall and a sickening crash as he hit the basement. Mathews looked over the edge. Paras lay immobile, sprawled awkwardly in a pool of blood. He was not moving. Paras was dead. Mathews' hands were clenched as he moved towards the door. He would confront Ayesha and tell her that he had killed her lover. He hoped that the court would give him a lenient sentence. Judges in India were known to be sympathetic to betrayed husbands. Thank God for misplaced Indian chauvinism.

He reached for the door handle and then froze. There was a brass knocker on the door that had not been there before. Blood drained from his face as he looked carefully at the door. This was not his house. He was on the wrong floor. He must have pressed the wrong button in the lift. With deepening dread, he peeped in through the magic eye. He could see the woman now. It was a tall shapely woman, but it was not Ayesha. She had not heard the scuffle on the landing. The door was solid wood and they had not made too much of noise in their struggle. They had fought silently, thought Mathews, just two protagonists in the ancient ritual of silently and fatally feuding over mating rights. The sounds of evening Mumbai traffic in the streets below would have muffled the sound further. He tiptoed back to the railing and peeked over the edge again. No one seemed to have seen or heard Paras fall. He stepped back carefully. Maybe he could escape. There was no motive to point towards his having committed the dastardly crime. He had murdered a man on a misunderstanding.

Mathew realized the significance of what he had done. If he were caught, he would rot behind bars for the rest of his life. Mathews' first impulse was to run. He would disappear from the world where he would be recognized. But what could he do. It was not an easy endeavor to create a new identity and he definitely had no expertise in these matters. He would be a wanted man and on the run. He could not confide in anyone. No one would harbour a murderer. The stakes were too high. Whatever he did, he would be on his own.

Mathews tried desperately to control his panic. If anyone saw him on the landing, the game would be up straightaway. Then he paused. There was no reason why anyone should suspect him. There was no motive. If he could remove any evidence and remain calm he might be able to escape suspicion. He whipped out his hand kerchief and wiped the railings. There would be no give away fingerprints. There was a drop of blood on the floor, which he wiped and cleaned again. Then he tiptoed down the stairs to his own floor, keeping close to the wall. No one saw him on the landing. He was safe till now. He focused on looking as normal as possible. When Ayesha opened the door, she should not suspect anything amiss. Not that she would notice anything. She generally looked through him, another necessary fixture in the house, that she could do without, but had got used to. He wondered if he should stick to the plan of taking her out. He would have to be really cold blooded to do that. Maybe, he would just tell her that he had not been feeling too well in the office.

He raised his finger to ring the doorbell to his house. In retrospect he could not imagine how he could have mistaken Paras' ornamented door for his own. No one would believe him if he told them the truth that he had been preoccupied and that the differences had not registered. He started in surprise and almost dropped his briefcase. The front door of his house was opening. He had the sinking feeling that it was Paras' ghost who had come for revenge and hurl him down the stairwell. The door opened and a thick set man almost bumped into him. Mathew recognized him. It was Shah. Shah was a business man and an art dealer. He had offered Ayesha a place for her work in his coming exhibition. Mathew had always been wary of him. Shah was wealthy and possibly had some underworld connections. But Ayesha was banking on him to project her work.

Mathew's mind was working furiously. If Shah left now, he would discover the body. The heat would turn on Mathews. The only way Mathews could survive without coming under the scanner was to stay out of the picture completely. If he were one of the suspects, something, some DNA analysis or such thing would nail him. He had to keep Shah in the house for a while. After the initial startle, they greeted each other. Mathew thought quickly. If Shah discovered the body first, he would smell a rat. He hustled Shah back in.

Shah seemed taken aback. Mathews had always been a little cold towards him earlier. Today he seemed insistent on being sociable. Shah seemed surprised at his sudden effusive affection. They walked into the dining hall as Mathews gratefully closed the door behind him. Let someone else discover the body. He had to keep Shah in the house till the initial uproar died down. Ayesha now emerged from her studio, looking flushed. She seemed a little surprised on seeing him. It was not surprising. Mathews was never home this early. Shah was shrugging his shoulders in resignation and Ayesha also seemed to relax. Ayesha was looking very attractive in her fluffed-up skirt and loose cotton blouse. "She has a glowing complexion", thought Mathews. 'How can you let him go, without having a drink?' he was chiding her. Shah settled on the sofa, while he fixed them both whiskeys. His hands were trembling. He could not hear any shouts from outside. Had Paras body been discovered yet?

'Cheers', he raised a toast to Shah. 'Cheers' responded Shah! "I brought some good news for Ayesha. I spoke to the director of the gallery. Ayesha's painting will be put up. I came to give her the news". Mathews know that Ayesha would be ecstatic. This was reason to celebrate. Ayesha had gone back inside her room. The exhibition could be the big break she was waiting for. This was something that she had always wanted. He felt a tinge of irritation. She should be bringing out the snacks and the wine. Where was she? Mathews got up from the sofa. He would have to do the entertaining himself. Ayesha had this habit of leaving him in the lurch. He was not even sure where the bowls were kept. There was a bottle of wine in the refrigerator. He was looking for a corkscrew. Shah offered to help him with the cork and Mathews handed him the bottle. Shah popped the cork with ease. Mathews was always envious of these 'men of the world' who were so adept at these social graces. This was one of the reasons why Ayesha had been unimpressed with him. He grimaced. He should have taken a finishing course in savoir-fare before he started dating and maybe even a crash course in lovemaking. Mathews grimaced at his own thoughts.

At that moment Ayesha emerged from her room. She had changed into Jeans and a 'T' shirt. Mathews was a little disappointed. Skirts were sensuous. A woman in a thin frilly skirt was infinitely more erotic than one in tight clothes. The Indian Sari could be exotic too. A well-worn chiffon accentuated a woman's sex appeal.

Ayesha had a great body and she moved well. He loved to watch her move around the room. He bit his lip in embarrassment as he saw Shah glancing at him. Mathews was still fascinated by her. It was tragic theat his appreciation was not reciprocated. He knew Ayesha considered him a bit of a wimp.

She would have to change into something a bit more formal if they were to go out. Shah could come with them to the Discotheque. He would look after Ayesha and make her feel good. Mathews grimaced at the thought that he was outsourcing entertaining his wife. That was an original thought. Let her be happy. It would be sad if they went out, just the two of them and they kept fighting. They could celebrate with Shah. He suddenly jolted himself back from his thoughts. He had just murdered a man and he was thinking of frivolities.

Ayesha was busy in the kitchen now and the aroma of fried sausages wafted in. Mathews poured out a glass of wine for her and carried it to the kitchen. His heart was still pounding violently. He peeped through the kitchen door. Ayesha was busy inspecting the sausages. She had sliced a pineapple to go with it. With her, everything had to be artistic and original. He crept up behind her and embraced her round the waist. Ayesha startled and dropped her spoon. 'Idiot' she muttered angrily, with a genuine disgust that made him feel small and inadequate. Mathew was taken aback. There was a time when she would have just melted into his arms. Unfortunately, that was only for a short time during their courtship before they had got married. Mumbling an apology, he hurried back into the living room. Shah had finished his drink and was admiring one of Ayesha's paintings on the wall. They had not heard any commotion outside.

Mathews resisted the temptation to go to the door on some pretext and peep down the stairwell. That could be a fatal giveaway. "Keep your cool", he muttered to himself. Ayesha had joined them in the living room.

They settled in their respective sofas. Only Shah, their guest, seemed to be completely at ease. He kept the conversation flowing with anecdotes on his experiences with various artistes, both famous and infamous. Ayesha was in splits and even Mathews was enjoying himself. A second bottle of wine had been opened. Emboldened by his second glass of wine, Mathews suggested that they go out for dinner and maybe visit a discotheque later. It was Ayesha who vetoed the idea. There was nice food at home. She was not too keen to go out. They persuaded Shah to stay back for dinner.

By the time dinner was over, it was nearing midnight. Mathew escorted Shah downstairs. He had almost forgotten the tragedy he had orchestrated a few hours ago. Suddenly he was enfolded in a cold grip of panic. His legs felt weak and he stumbled as he walked out of the house and towards the lift. Ayesha had stayed back to put away the plates and glasses for the maid to wash the next day. Shah held his arm to steady him. "Too much wine" Mathews mumbled as he struggled to regain his composure as they got into the lift and moved to the basement. The basement was bustling with activity. There was a police jeep downstairs and the area around the stairwell had been cordoned off. "What happened?' Shah enquired of a policeman who gave them a sharp look and then looked away. "Some one fell down and died". The policeman was quite curt. "Was it an accident?' Shah was being persistent. "How do I know, only the investigation will tell us", was the cop's comment. No one was paying any special interest to him. If the cops were efficient, they could easily identify people who had come into the complex around the time of the man's fall. If they pursued that line of investigation, Mathew's could be in trouble.

"I wonder who the unfortunate blighter in a hurry was" quipped Shah. He was looking at Mathew. "Must be cleaner or a vendor', said Mathew, as he guided Shah away from the scene and towards his car. "Who else would be using the stairs?" Shah had parked his SUV in the visitor's parking lot which was towards the rear of the building. It was a flashy affair, very muscular looking, with chunky tires and a high cabin. He swung himself into the driving seat and drove off with a screech of his tires. Mathews waited as the car stopped at the sentry post for the boom barrier to rise. He wondered how he had got into the complex. He would have telephoned Ayesha and she must have authorized the gate to let him in. Mathew took the lift back home, deliberately avoiding the group at the stair wall. He was tired and could easily do or say something which could ignite suspicion. Ayesha was already in bed and pretending to sleep. This was her standard way of avoiding intimacy. Her coldness suited Mathews tonight. If Ayesha had asked any questions, she would have caught on that something was amiss. He did not conceal stress well and something he did or said would have given the game away. Ayesha with her woman's intuition would have immediately caught on that something was amiss.

He was emotionally drained and physically exhausted. It was fortunate that the evening had not gone as planned. He would probably have passed out in the hotel. Mathew retired to the guest bed room. Over the past year, they had come to a tacit no touch agreement of sorts. It had hurt a bit at first when they shifted to separate bed rooms. Ayesha had made it clear that she preferred to sleep alone. Mathew tossed and turned in bed trying desperately to blot out memories of the evening. A breeze blew in through the window. Would Paras ghost waft in and strangle him when he slept. There was a crucifix in the dressing table. Mathew kept the crucifix under his pillow and with the night light still on closed his eyes. He slept in fits and starts for a while. He checked the wall clock. It was three in the morning. Soon it would be light. At 5.30, the maid would be seeing ring the bell and the milkman would be coming. He got up. There was some pending correspondence he had to make. He logged in on his computer. On a whim, he tried to plan escape out of the country or may be just migrate under an alias to the Andaman Islands. He wondered about Ayesha. Was there something going between her and Shah. Shah had been with her alone in the house. Ayeshas bedroom door was closed. He walked into her work room. This was where she had entertained Shah in the evening. The paintings on the wall seemed to sneer at him. He lay down on her mat. It was soft and feathery. The satiny pillow was cozy and comfortable. As he shifted the pillow he noticed something pink beneath. It was Ayeshas pink innerwear. What was it doing under her pillow.

The truth struck him with blinding clarity. It was suddenly clear to him. He had been right in his assessment of Ayesha's infidelity. But he had killed the wrong man. He was a murderer. If he escaped detection, he would let Ayesha do whatever she wanted to. The bell rang. It was the maid.

Mathews had had a sudden twinge of fear before he opened the door. Had the cops come for him. The maid walked in agog with excitement. She was full of the story. Ayesha had got up too and was sitting at the table. Thhey listened as the maid narrated the events. Paras had been brutally murdered in the basement by unknown assailants who had broken every bone in his body. The police had arrested the model, who had been found in Paras's house. The premise was that some jealous lover of her's had murdered Paras. The story was right, thought Mathew – only the script had got the characters all mixed up.

Mark Antony

"**D**o you really expect us to look after you"? The rasping note in the lady's voice kindled Marc's dormant pride. It had not been realistic to expect that he would be welcome. Not when the chips were down. Inside, he could hear the sounds of a party in progress. He must have slept off. Evicted from his own house by his creditors, he had cycled down, hoping to be a part of the wedding party while he collected his many thoughts and meagre assets. He was hungry and needed a place to lay his head. The sprawling estate of his father's cousin had many outhouses and there was never any shortage of food at a wedding.

He remembered the warm welcomes he had received there when he had visited with his father. His father had been a man of respect. Father's death, a series of bad decisions in matrimony and investments and a dubious reputation had brought him to this nadir. Marc was quick to regain his composure. "On no, I cannot stay for dinner, we have a college get together tonight". By pretending to misunderstand his tormentor, he was trying to absolve himself of the indignity of imminent eviction.

He looked at the irate aunt who was viewing him with incredulous suspicion. "They have booked a cottage for me". He was going into too many details. A dead giveaway. The tack in the conversation had brought him some time and he walked purposely through the hall. He knew all the guests or at least most of them. They were avoiding looking him in the eye. They all seemed acutely aware of his impending, abject, inevitable humiliation. He glanced around while he kept walking towards the front door. There was no sympathetic empathy in anyones eyes. A few aunts looked embarrassed. Their husbands scrowled. His uncle stood there with the most violent scrowl of all.

An astute physician in his time, Dr Cherian had evolved into a major player in the health care industry. He ran a string of highly profitable and exclusive hospitals and ayurvedic health resorts across the country. His face was stern as he prepared to snub Marc. But Marc had other plans. Smugly, he walked over and briskly apologised for being unable to stay. Turning sharply on his heels, he walked out, ears stinging in shame as he heard a suppressed snigger from one of the guests. He hopped back on his cycle, feeling the warm flow of tears down his parched cheeks. It was dark and he was grateful for the anonymity it offered him on the road. With his teary red eyes anyone who saw him would think he was a drunk. Maybe, he could pretend to be drunk and lie on the roadside. There was more dignity in being drunk than in being homeless.

Without thinking, he cycled back towards his old house. It was a familiar route, one that he had pedalled down decades ago as young man with an apparent bright future. As he neared his destination the realisation that he would be turned off at the gate set in. The guards, appointed by the new owners had been given specific instructions to keep him off the grounds. They were from a security agency in town and would have no sympathy towards him. He had seen the homeless being beaten with lathis when they tried to find shelter. He was out of options.

 There was a mud track which led to the back of his father's estate. He turned his cycle down the path. He could see lights on in the outhouse. This would be where the security chap was resting. Marc parked his cycle under a tree and proceeded on foot, careful not to step on any twigs. A crescent moon supported by a full cast of stars gave him just enough light to walk without stumbling. He was near the corner of his house, near the room that had been his through his childhood and till today. There were stairs that lead to the terrace guarded by a wicket gate. He stepped over the creaky gate.

There was a room on the terrace, a room that had been made for Thankan the watchman, but had never been used. He eased the door open. He knew his way around. Silently he made his way to the bare bed in the corner. Lying down, he closed his eyes. In a minute he was fast asleep. He must have slept for a couple of hours.

 The discomfiture of gnawing hunger and the urgency of whispered voices in the room below woke him up. Marc lay still. The dread of being discovered and dispossessed of his resting place made him breathe slow and shallow. The sounds were clearer now. The frenzied heavy breaths of the burly security guard and the mumbled entreaties of the woman gave way to a silence as damp as a monsoon night. Marc lay still.

He was more afraid than ever. If the security guard caught him now, he was dead. Marc had no business to be here and the guard would murder him to guard his own secrets. He recognised the woman's voice. Tanku, the washer woman lived with her young son in a brick and mud hut on the ten cents of land gifted by Marc's father. An orphan, she had grown up in their house, helping out in the cooking and cleaning.

They had sent her to school, but she dropped out within months. She ran away with a fish monger when she was sixteen, returning unrepentant and penniless three years later with a babe in her arms. Marc's father had got the hut built in the small plot of land he gifted her.

He heard the front door open and close. There were no more voices heard. Marc closed his eyes and drifted off to sleep again. He woke up before sunrise. There was a small pond in the gounds. He washed himself,used the corner of his Dhoti to wipe himself dry and mounted his cycle. On an impulse, he cycled to the rail station. The lot was always full of cycles of workers who commuted to work at Kochi. Buying himself a return ticket he checked his finances. There was enough money for food for the day. There was a little money in a bank acount he could access with his ATM card. He would need to find some work, and keep his finances stable. The passenger train he was in would take over two hours to reach Kochi. He climbed on the broken uncushioned wooden baggage bunk and dozed off.

At Kochi, he walked down the MG road, waiting for shops to open, asking for work. Folks did not know him here and the anonymity suited him. It was almost midday before he got hired. The Sikh Gentleman who ran the motor spare parts shop was not as suspicious of him as the locals. He worked as a handyman, running errands, bringing down boxes from the warehouse to the store and helping customers with their merchandise. The man gave him money for a hearty lunch. He managed to catch the night passenger, sleeping again on the wooden bunk. Collecting his cycle, he returned to his hideout on the terrace. He barely woke up when he heard the security man with Tanku. He was up in the early hours and back to the Sardar's shop in the morning.

 Marc settled in to a charitably mindnumbing balm of a routine. There was comfort in the exhaution and he was making a little money. He hated Sundays. The shop was closed and he had no place to go. There was no anonymity on a Sunday. Those who were on the roads out were there on their own volition and in their own time. They were more likely to recognise you and ask questions. He made the trip to Kochi on Sundays too, but had to spend his time loitering around, which was more tiring than working.

One night when Marc returned to his hideout, he got the surprise of his life. There was a small neatly wrapped packet of food wrapped in a banana leaf. Tapioca and fish were his favourite combo. His first emotion was fear. The meal must belong to someone and that someone could arrive at any moment. After initial consternation he realised that the meal was for him. Tanku must have realised that he was sleeping there at night. He opened the packet. The food was still warm and the recipe was distictively Tanku's. Tanku would have realised that someone was using the loft as a hideout.She must have guessed it was him and cooked him his favourite dish.

 The security guard and his benefactor were at it again in his room. Marc guessed that Tanku was possibly trying to earn a little extra money. He was just a bit concerned for her safety. The little dinner pack in a banana leaf became a daily routine. He did not want to push his luck, trying to thank Tanku.

One of the Autorikshaw drivers who plied the Nedumbassery airport area got him employment for Sundays. While waiting for his battery to be changed, the driver told Marc how difficult it was to find someone to drive autorikshaws on a Sunday. Most drivers wanted the day off to spend with their families. Marc offered to take on the job and his problem of idle Sundays was solved. His driving skills had not rusted from the days when they had their own car. He would pick up the autorikshaw from George sar, the auto owners's houseand go to the Angamaly railway station close by. With air travel becoming more universal, there were many folks who came by rail and took a rickshaw to the airport. The route was a lucrative one and the customers were infrequent passengers whom one could fleece with impunity.

Every rikshaw driver on this route had cultivated a pet story. Marc loved the one about his daughter going to college. He would choose the college depending on the probable occupation of the customer. The general theme was that his daughter had got admission and a scholarship based on her merit, but needed a little extra money to pay for her accomodation. There were no requests for money. The statement that this was the reason, he had to work on Sundays, prevented even the most hardened of travellors from protesting too much when he charged them three times the fair fare. Air travellors were especially supersticious. Up at thirty thousand feet an engine or software malfunction or a terrorist with a bomb could annihilate them all. The passenger would be keen on appeasing the gods by contributing to a noble cause. Marc made a lot of extra money even after paying five hundred rupees to George Sar in the evening.

The Sardar shop owner helped Marc start a new bank account and soon Marc had a little stash in the local microfinance branch. He was developing a fresh identity now and did not want to stash his new earnings in the old bank. He made plans to meet up with Thanku after he had a little more money. He would take a day off and visit her with gifts for her and her son. He would move out of his hideout after this and possibly find a small place of his own elsewhere. Maybe, if he could make enough money to rescue her from her need to moonshine with security guards, he would propose marriage to her.

 He had his aspirations and plans now and he started working harder. The Autorikshaw was soon earning him more every Sunday than a week at the Sardar's shop. He continued working for them however out of a sense of loyalty. Besides, the pickings on weekdays were not as lucrative as on a Sunday. The regular office goers would cry foul if he tried to fleece them. He would drive the rikshaw till the wee hours of Monday morning and then catch an hour or two of sleep at the railway station before going to the shop for his days work.

Then one day, Marc became an accesssory to a murder. He had dropped off a flight attendent on duty and was howering around, hoping to get a client before the airport security chased him off the airport perimeter. Thampi, was a local goon with political pretensions who extorted money from shopkeepers and factory owners. When he saw Thampi coming towards him with a tourist in tow, his first impulse was to get away. Thampi however had seen him and gestured for him to stop.

In the rikshaw, Thampi was feeding the tourist, one con line after another in broken English. Marc realised that he was planning to rob him. He could try and feign a breakdown, but then Thampi had made him take a dark side road on which there was no one. If Marc tried any stunts there would be not one, but two victims tonight. Marc kept driving, following the goon's instructions. There was an old abandoned bridge over the river. It was considered unsafe for vehicles, and there usually was a 'Road Blocked' sign. Today the sign was missing.

Cyclists and local pedestrians still used the bridge as a shortcut to the highway. Thampi ordered him to drive across. Halfway down the bridge was the road block sign across the road. Marc recognised the well-built man, Kuttan, an accomplise of Thampi's, waving them to a stop. As Marc stopped, Kuttan reached across and yanked the key out of the ignition, abusing him. With the tourist's attention focussed on them, it was a simple matter for Thampi to slip a noose around the man's neck. Kuttan joined Thampi as they yanked the struggling man who was now blue in the face out of the rickshaw. A knife had mysteriously appeared in Kuttans hands now. Marc kept sitting in the Rickshaw muttering his prayers. He heard a horrible muffled cry from the man and then there was silence. A few minutes later, there was a splash as the tourist's dead body hit the water. Marc was trembling, waiting for his turn. They made him carry the 'Road blocked' sign to it's original site. Thampi and Kuttan were in the rickshaw now. They had the man's bags and jacket. They made him drive to a lodge near the toddy shop. He was surprised when they thrust some money into his hands and told him to get lost. His hands shaking, he drove to the railway station. He checked the notes they had given him. There were ten five-hundred-rupee notes. It was blood money. He was scared of going to the cops. They would fleece him and pin the murder on him. If he managed to convince some honest bigwig about what really happened, Thampi's friends would slit his throat. He sat in the rikshaw the rest of the night before handing the vehicle back to George Sar.

The rest of the week was a dizzy whirl. He expected the police to nab him any day. If they traced the rickshaw, George Sar had both his licence number and the address of the shop he worked at during the week. He decided against running away. It would direct suspicion to him. He kept scanning the papers. There was no news of the tourist's murder. Finally on Thursday he read in a tabloid about a man's body washed ashore on one of the local beaches. Police suspected that he was part of a drug ring. The murder was blamed on gang rivalries.

Marc was in the clear. After the incident on Sunday, he had decided to give up rikshaw driving. He soon changed his mind. Now that the finger of suspicion was pointing elsewhere, it would be foolish to get attention on himself by absconding. He was at George Sar's house next Sunday, collecting the auto keys as if nothing had happened. He kept a wary eye open for Thampi or Kuttan and avoided hanging out near the arrival foyer of the airport.

After the shop closed on Monday, he boarded the train for Kottayam. He had decided to stay back on Tuesday morning and call on Tanku. He was hoping that she would agree to marry him. His stash of money was reasonable now. They could have a future together. The excitement and anticipation prevented him from sleeping. There was a discarded newspaper lying on the bunk Idly, he turned the pages. Suddenly he froze. On the fourth page, there was a photograph of him. It was a lookout notice from the Kerala police.

He looked around warily. No one was watching him. Fortunately, the photograph was an old one. No one who looked at the young executive looking chap in the photograph would suspect that the unshaven manual labourer sitting on the bunk was the same person. As he read the news item, he froze. Tanku had been raped and murdered in the loft of his old house. According to the police, it was an open and shut case. The erstwhile owner Marc, had lured her to the loft and raped her. When she tried to raise an alarm, he had slit her throat. The train had reached Kottayam station. He warily approached the cycle stand. There were no cops in sight. He picked up the cycle and cycled towards the bus stand from where Bangalore bound buses plied. He propped the bike against a wall and went and sat with passengers waiting for the many buses which would leave through the night.

Marc slept under one of the benches. A cold rage was coursing through him. He had a burning urge to go and butcher the security guard who had brutally murdered Tanku. He was sure that the police would be watching the house. He would be nabbed if he went anywhere near. The murder he had witnessed near the airport had steeled his resolve. He would have to forgo the identity of Marc for ever. He swore that he would avenge Tanku's death. Wisdom prevailed.Revenge would have to wait.

Leaving the bicycle at the bus station he walked down and caught the early morning train to Kochi. If the cops identified the cycle as his, they would assume that he was hiding at Bangalore. He would not return to Kottayam. Marc concocted a story about his family going to stay with his inlaws at Trivandrum for a while. The Sardar was only too happy to let him sleep on the premises as a security man. There had been a spate of robberies at Kochi and most shop owners were hiring some kind of security. The arrangement worked out well. He was free on Sunday. He told the shop owner he visited his family on Sunday. He would take Sundays off on the pretext of visiting his family and drive the ricketty rickshaw to augment his income.

The Sardars shop was on a busy bylane in the metropolis. The road was deserted after the shops closed at night. There was only one residential apartment on the street. There was a jeweller's shop next to the Sardar's spare part depot. 'Janki Brothers' was a famous jewellery line which had outlets all over the country. This particular outlet was operated by the Oxford educated son of the youngest of the brothers. A reluctant recruit to the jewellery trade, Bhushan now stayed in the apartment over the shop with his wife Lara, a pretty English girl he had met while studying in the UK. Marc had helped them to set up house when they moved in. He had supervised proceedings, controlling the extortive organised labour gangs. He had helped move and install exquisite furniture the young wife had chosen for their new house. Bhushan had given him a nice gift in cash and had guided him on how to invest his savings.

It was well past midnight, one Wednesday night when Bhushan woke up. He had heard a woman scream. His first thought was that he was having another nightmare. After Tanku's murder, he had these horrible dreams of Tanku begging for his help while the security guard strangled her. In every dream, his cowardice had prevented him from trying to save her. Then he heard the muffled sound of a woman's cry again. It was coming from Bhushan's house. He sprang to his feet. In the dark, he could see an open window. Robbers had broken in. Bhushan had refused to hire night security guards. There was no place for them to stay. Besides, once, the jewellery shop was locked from the inside it was virtually an impregnable fortress. The only way to open the jewelry shop without a cacophony of alarms being set off was from the inside. Bhushan opened the shop himself every day, while the day guards and workers waited outside. He would come down the stairwell from the flat and switch off the alarms before opening the door. He had shown Marc a licensed revolver he kept by the bedside. The young man had been too sure of his capability to protect himself and his family.

Marc used the water pipe to support himself as he scaled the wall. He found his footing on the parapet, reached the open window and peeped in. A street light provided a glimmer of illumination. He saw Bhushan's body lying on the floor. Marc padded across to the prostrate form. There was a small pool of blood around the man's head. He was deeply unconsious, but breathing. Marc could hear muffled voices downstairs. He heard an anguished subdued moan of a woman downstairs. He checked the dressing table near the bed. Bhushan's revolver was lying there. Fortunately, the robbers had not seen it. Bhushan must have been surprised by the robbers when he went to investigate some sound from near the window. Marc checked the revolver. It was loaded. He had fired one before, when his father, a rifle enthusiast had taken him to the range. Keeping the revolver close to his side, he climbed softly down the stairway. There was a dull light of a torch coming from the shop. He could hear someone breaking the glass and the clink of jewellery being dumped into a bag.

Suddenly he heard another sound. A womans muffled cries and the laboured breathing of a man coming from the corner of the room. A cold anger ceased him. The nightmares of Tanku were still emblazoned in his subconsious. He crept forward. He could see them both now. He stood up and at close range shot the man robbing the ornaments through the head. As the man fell, Marc recognised him. It was Thampi. He turned towards the man on the floor. Kuttan had got up in a panic, while Bhushans wife crawled away crying, gathering her torn night clothes around her. Marc shot Kuttan in the genitals and as the man rolled around, screaming in agony he waited, cold as a statue. The man's cries became feeble as he bled to death. Marc stepped forward and fired another bullet into the man's head. He helped the girl back up to her flat, and then dialled for an ambulance and the cops. The girl rang up her father-in-law and in a few minutes the flat was swarming with people.

Bhushan was taken to hospital where he needed an operation in the middle of the night. The girl was taken to a resort in an undisclosed location by her mother in law. They would keep her out of the glare of publicity while she got over the trauma. Everyone seemed to forget about Marc. He was taken into custody, by the police. They initially treated him like a hero. When he told them, who he was, the scenario changed. There was soon a hypothesis that he was part of the gang. Marc already had the murder of Tanku on his record and there was no one to clear his name.

Newspapers carried reports of a three-man gang who attacked Bhushan and his wife. One of the gang members, the newspapers stated, was Marc Antony, the murderer of Tanku. Tabloids screamed for early justice. Marc had tried to defend himself, but there was no one in the police station or prison who would listen to him. The only person who could protect him in this case was Lara. She was esconsed in a protective coccoon by her powerful in-laws who assured her that everything was being taken care of. The official line was that she was not even in the flat when the robbery occurred.

The day of the trial was drawing near. The death sentence seemed likely in the Tanku murder case. There was enough circumstantial evidence to nail him. The trial received plenty of publicity. Details of the robbery and murder were hazy and the motive behind his killing Kuttan and Thampi unclear. The prosecution would gloss over the facts, giving the impression of a ruthless monster, murdering at will. As Marc could not afford a lawyer, the defence was a farce. The press had a field day, with theories of drug rings and foreign money adding to the masala. A bunch of political activists assaulted him after the trial, as he was being escorted in handcuffs to jail. The police took their time to intervene, by which time he was badly beaten and required hospitalisation.

Bhushan had spent almost a month in hospital. He was almost fully recovered. He had no memory of the incident and Lara, who could communicate with him, could speak to him only on skype. Lara had been insulated from all press coverage of the incident. The day Bhushan was discharged from hospital, he joined Lara at the health resort.

Lara and Bhushan were given a seperate cottage at the resort. It was in this cottage that Lara chanced upon a magazine which reported the trial of Marc Antony. Marc was to be discharged from hospital that day. The judge would pronounce the sentence the day after. The enormity of the injustice sank into Lara. The man who had saved them was being punished. She realised that her in-laws had let it happen to insulate her from the glare and humiliation of public scrutiny. She told Bhushan that a friend of hers was coming from the United Kingdom and that she had to meet her. Taking the car, she drove towards Kochi.

Lara reached the court room just as Marc was being marched in. Marcs arm was in plaster and a bandage covered his head. Their eyes met. Marc looked at her with consternation. Why was she here? He had often wondered why she had not come forward to defend him. He had concluded that she too felt that he was part of the gang. In her traumatised state, the full sequence of events had probably not registered. He had wanted to explain his actions to her. He owed it to Tanku to clear his name. Now it was too late. The court rose as the judge entered. The judge was a senior man, respected for his honesty and feared for his ruthlessness while dealing with criminals. He had picked up the typed verdict and was starting to read when there was an interruption.

"Your Honour. I have to make a statement". It was Lara. The judge glared at her. He recognised her. She was Bhushan's wife. He allowed her to proceed. If it were something frivolous, he would have jailed her for contempt of court.

Lara's first line brought out hushed whispers all over the courtroom. "I was there on the night of the robbery and this man saved me". She was pointing towards Marc. The judge called her forward to the witness stand from where she narrated her story, skipping no detail, a catch in her voice the only reflection of her emotional turmoil. The press which was present in strength to record the verdict went wild, recording, filming and taking notes. At the end of it the judge deffered his verdict, ordering the prosecution to reopen the case in view the fresh evidence.

Lara's father-in-law heard of the drama in court. He was waiting outside when Lara exited. He was red faced,but wanted to make amends. While sheltering Lara, he would have rewarded Marc. The public outcry against Marc on the Tanku murder, steeled his resolve not to interfere. Now he chose to make amends. He hired a top team of private investigators to reopen the Tanku case.

The findings were startling. At post mortem, DNA samples had been collected from Tanku's private parts, but they had not been matched. A sample had been preserved. The investigators proved that the sample did not match Marc. The security guard got wind of the ongoing trend of events and absconded. He was never to be traced again. Shamefacedly, under pressure from the influential Janki family the police dropped the case against Marc. He was a free man again. The Janki's appointed him manager of their outlet at Kochi. Bhushan had no interest in the shop now. He and Lara set up a chain of luxury resorts across India. Lara tied a Rakhi on Marc. He was almost a family member now.

Marc now stayed in Bhushan's old house. He was unwaveringly loyal to his new family, driven by a passion to excel. In five years, Marc managed to get two more outlets open at Kochi, one of which dealt exclusively with designer jewellery and accessories. This was Lara's idea and it was a great success. Bhushan was now acquiring a chain of hospitals. He would develop them into speciality centres and dabble in medical tourism.

 It was at a party thrown by the Jamki's for directors of the recently acquired hospitals that he came across his uncle Dr Cherian and his wife. Marc was family and he could see his relatives cringe when he spoke to them. The lady recovered first. "Uncle was so upset that day after you left. He really wanted you to stay on". Marc nodded kindly. Yes. He was sorry. He had been busy.

Raghunath of Rajbhavan.

Chapter1   The Rajbhavan

Raghunath Thankappan was the manager of the government house at Kottayam. His father had been the estate supervisor of the British viceroy. After the British left, the Indian government had taken over the viceroy's bungalow and property. The establishment was now called the government house or Rajbhavan. It was a sort of weekend getaway for politicians and senior policemen. The tariffs were low and the décor and ambience of the Victorian structure excellent.

Raghunath had been selected as caretaker of the estate by the state government. There had been some initial opposition to his appointment. This, after all, was a government job and there were enough unemployed politicians who were not averse to accepting government dole. Better sense however had prevailed. Raghunath, like his father before him, had grown up in the estate. There were gardens, which they had managed to nurture, even with the limited resources at their disposal. If Raghunath and his family moved out of the premises, the bungalow and its gardens would fall into ruin. What Raghunath did not know was that these arguments and the ultimate result had been influenced by his wife Kalpana. She pawned her gold chain and made an appropriate deposit in the party coffers. Justice triumphed. Raghu got the appointment.

The Rajbhavan building was an elegant structure of teakwood and granite. The structure was on a raised platform supported by wood and cement pillars. The British always constructed their houses in the colonies propped up on pillars. This kind of structure kept away snakes and creepy crawlies. The structure was imposing and the high tiled roof kept the interiors cool. It helped too, that the building was on top of a hill. Cool breeze from the sea, which was barely visible as a distant glimmer in the horizon, blew through the wide curtained windows. There were clumps of bamboo around the estate. In the centre of the garden was a greenhouse. This was a glass structure that housed a variety of tropical and other plants. The viceroy's wife had collected these in her travels around the country.

A deep stone well on the premises gave sparkling cool water for the house and garden. Raghu was justifiably proud of the garden and greenhouse. He kept both in excellent repair. The building too was well maintained, with the teak wood structures polished to perfection. Indeed all visiting dignitaries including the president, stayed at the Rajbhavan when they visited this part of the country. At other times, the estate house was a favorite locale for clandestine political meetings. At a telephone call from the authorities, Raghu would get the conference hall ready and call in Velu, the official cook.

By evening, the cars would roll in. Some of the faces were familiar, from newspaper photographs. A small posse of plainclothes policemen would hover around the premises to keep any newspaper men at bay.

Invariably, the meetings would go on till late in the night. Dinner would be rice and Karimeen fish curry that Velu would lovingly prepare. Velu's virtuosity with fish preparations was legendary. Irrespective of what transpired in the meeting, they all went back with happy faces.

Raghunath's wife Kalpana was a very hard-working lady. She supervised the décor and the upkeep of the bungalow. The dhobi, who stayed on the premises, was kept busy. The furniture maintenance and polishing teams had to earn their wages. There was no lazing off with Kalpana around. Kalpana was the interior decorator, chief hostess and accountant. Raghu's passion was the garden and the outhouses, which he restored and maintained with diligence and pride. The landscaping had been planned superbly by the old viceroy's wife. With the garden restored and the flowers in bloom the place became a favourite picnic spot. Families would visit the government house premises with picnic hampers during the evening hours, when the garden was kept open and the entry was free of charge.

Chapter 2   The Summit

It was July and the monsoon had been particularly harsh this season. The government house took the battering of the seasons well. The British, as usual had constructed a solid edifice. There was no seepage of water and the teak wood construct had never lost its sheen. There was a covered path leading from Raghu's house to the main bungalow. Raghu had finished his lunch and was waiting for a respite in the torrential outflow to get back to his office.Through the angled curtain of rain, he could see Ravi the peon waving frantically to him. There was a telephone call for him in the office and from Ravi's antics he guessed that the caller was an important person.

Braving the sheet of rain that deluged the passage, Raghu tucked up his white mundu. Pointing his umbrella at the monsoon barrage, he scampered across to the main block. He hurried to the telephone. It was the assistant director of tourism. Tonight, the chief minister and a select few of the cabinet would be using the bungalow for a high level meeting. There was a visitor from Delhi, whose identity was being kept a secret. Raghu sighed. Central elections were just round the corner and these meets were inevitable. He wondered who the visitor from Delhi was. Could it be Maninder, that scion from a royal family, who had taken it upon himself to revamp the party and to route out corruption?

Raghu swung into action. The rain had subsided for now. Velu was summoned. Karimeen was ordered from the local market. It would be delivered to the estate within an hour. Chicken and paneer would also be delivered from the departmental store in town. Kalpana would have to supervise the vegetarian cooking. A surprising number of north Indians were vegetarians. Velu's culinary expertise had been honed, further up the food chain.

Kalpana ensured that the curtains were changed and that bottles of mineral water were kept in the refrigerator. By convention, they never stocked alcoholic beverages at the bungalow. Raghu had learned from experience that it was better to let the secretaries of the visiting dignitaries order whatever was desired from the local five star hotels.

The motorcade rolled in by nine at night. There were two covered security vehicles escorting five limousines. Raghu smiled when the occupants of the first car got out. His guess had been right. It was Maninder, the new superstar of Indian politics along with the chief minister. As the other cars disgorged their occupants, Raghu was impressed. There were some prominent industrialists and at least one movie star in the group. Someone had got together a dream team. Maninder must have done it.

Raghu had discarded his normal mundu and kurta for a trouser, shirt and tie. He welcomed them at the foyer and led the group into the conference hall. He signaled to the waiter. Lime juice and coconut water that had been prepared for the occasion and were served now.

The chief minister's secretary went with Raghu to his office. This was more than a meeting. The VIP's would need to be contactable. A telephone exchange was set up and telephones in the guest rooms activated. Raghu was impressed. Normally the telephone department would take a week to respond to a complaint and a year to issue a new connection. Four VIP rooms were to be made ready. Liveried attendants from a government agency had drawn up in a mini bus, along with special crockery and cutlery. This was going to be more than a meeting. This was a summit that would last at least three days.

Dinner was served after the evenings deliberations. Maninder was presiding over the ruminations. Raghu was not sure as to how the meeting went or what the agenda under discussion was. They all concurred that the dinner was great and that the ambience could not have been better. Velu's Karimeen and Kalpana's Thorans received universal acclaim. There had been no liquor served tonight. Both Maninder and the chief minister were teetotalers and the industrialists had too much work to be completed before the next day's meet. A few of the others were planning some serious after dinner drinking at the lagoon. This was a bar in town owned by the health minister's nephew. After dinner Maninder and the chief minister retired to their separate rooms. Two of the industrialists also stayed back. The rest of the group would be put up in various luxury hotels around town. Raghu could retire to his room only around midnight.

At five in the morning he vaguely heard the alarm clock ring. Kalpana was up and she would ensure that the guests got their bed tea and breakfast in time. Raghu could afford to sleep a while longer. The first of the days meetings was scheduled for ten o'clock. At six am, Raghu was shaken awake by Kalpana. Maninder had expressed a desire to speak to him. It took Raghu 15 minutes to get ready. He hoped groggily that it was not for a complaint.

Raghu was not at his best in the early hours of the morning. When he reached VIP room no 1, Maninder was in his track suit, cooling off after his morning run. "I was jogging around the garden. The outhouses and landscaping seemed quite fascinating", said Maninder. He seemed to be in a good mood. Could Mr Raghunath escort him around the grounds and tell him a bit about the history of the place? Raghu glowed with pride. The garden was his first love.

He escorted Maninder around the grounds. The remnants of colonial splendour wee well preserved. There was the old marble dance floor that overlooked the paddy fields and the Meenachil river. The field and the river were a good thousand feet below. They could see a few boats on the river, their occupants barely visible at this distance. Adjacent to the dance floor was a small stage, where the best music bands and most entrancing dance troupes had performed. The great lawn was still splendid, with a few palm trees and thorny bougainvilleas framing the periphery.

From the lawn, there was a path that led to the green house. There was a whole section of exotic tropical plants. There were cacti and lilies, orchids and roses. The glass of the green house was kept clean by a cleverly designed sprinkler system.

They left the greenhouse. The outhouses were still well maintained. Raghu showed Maninder the secret tunnel, which lead from the garden to a secret chamber under the viceroy's room. Near this was a stable. It was here that the viceroy always kept a couple of saddled horses. These could spirit him and his family to safety, in case the bungalow was ever besieged. Parts of the tunnel had fallen in and the roots of giant banyan trees had created an invincible lattice work within the tunnel. "So, I will not be able to escape in case the paparazzi land up" said Maninder. They both laughed.

The estate was walled in by a stone wall around ten feet high. In a few places, holes had been broken in the walls by local toughs who wanted a secluded place to gamble at cards. Some repairs had been done, but they would need a major project to restore the walls to their former glory.

Maninder glanced at his watch. It was half past nine. They returned to the bungalow. During breakfast, Maninder quizzed Kalpana. He was surprised to hear that she had completed her MA in economics, before settling down as a housewife. She was however putting her education to good use, maintaining the Rajbhavan accounts. She also took classes in a private college twice a week. He enquired about the couples children. There were two boys ten and twelve years of age. They were both in hostel at the military school at Ranchi.

The day's meetings started. Maninder obviously meant business. His party was almost certain to win the coming elections. The core group was discussing plans for the nation's rebuilding. Overall, the summit was a grand success. Maninder returned to Delhi after three days. The chief minister and the rest of the group left later in the evening. Raghu was surprised that the press had not got wind of the group's meet. If they had, they must have been under orders to keep the issue hushed.

The summit was over. Raghu and his team would need a couple of days to sort out the bills and accounts. Raghu's children would be coming home for their holidays in a week. They had strict discipline enforced at the school and looked forward to their holidays to create as much ruckus as they could. Raghu had promised the kids an expedition to the Thekkady wild life preserve. He had already booked the government tourist bungalow in the reserve forest.

Chapter 3   The Children have a Holiday

The elections were only two weeks away. There had been no more meetings in the government house after the summit. Raghu guessed that the politicians were too busy in their own constituencies now. An IPS officer from Delhi had checked in at the government house for a week on holiday. They stayed at the bungalow and headed out daily in a hired car to visit Alleppy and Vaikom and other spots of tourist interest.

 The children, Sumant and Hemant, came in by the Trivandrum express from Delhi. Raghu had hired a cab to pick them up at the station. The taxi belonged to Kunju, who was a friend of the family. Kunju's son was a drunkard. Despite his failing eyesight and health, Kunju still plied his old ambassador taxi to eke out a living. He enjoyed errands like this. With known customers, he got an opportunity to unwind and to discuss current affairs. The boys were glad to see old Kunju and his familiar rattly car. They reached home for lunch. Kalpana would not be able to accompany them to Thekkady. Someone had to stay back to look after to supervise the Rajbhavan accounts and affairs. There was no one else who was honest and capable enough to be entrusted with the responsibility.

The boys had a memorable holiday. The guest house was in shambles, but the locale was exotic. Every morning, herds of elephants trooped by their window, on their way to the reservoir. Deer pranced around the lawns, oblivious to the children's presence. The forest department's jeep drove them around the sanctuary. Sumant had received a camera for his eleventh birthday. He had always been scared of animals, especially of dogs. Raghu hoped that the exposure to wildlife would change all that. The boys excitedly captured the essence of their holiday on film.

Chapter 4   New Jobs for Raghu and Kalpana

When they returned home, Kalpana had a letter for Raghu. It had come in the official mail. Raghu tore open the envelope. It was from Maninder. Could Raghu fly down to Delhi the next week, after the election fever settled down? There were certain issues Maninder wished to discuss with him. Once Raghu finalized the dates, he was to ring up Maninder's secretary. The secretary would arrange the tickets and organise transportation.

The elections went as predicted. Maninder's party had won with an overwhelming majority. Maninder had declined to take on the mantle of Prime minister. Raghu flew to Delhi with the boys. After putting the boys on the train to Jhansi, he was taken to the party headquarters. His appointment with Maninder was the last in the day and he had time to freshen up in his hotel room. It was almost nine when the secretary ushered him into the young leader's office. Maninder rose to receive him. A peon brought in two plates with a large pizza and cokes. Maninder would be having a working dinner with him. Over pizza and coke, the two chatted. After the initial pleasantries Maninder came straight to the point. Would Raghu take over as the director of Kerala tourism? A senior portfolio in the department of handicrafts had been vacant for a while. If Kalpana were willing, she could be offered the job.

Raghu was taken aback. Maninder reassured him that all would be fine. The appointment was at the government's discretion and with some application the couple would be able to deliver the goods. Maninder and Raghu discussed the issues and shared their vision of Indian tourism before retiring for the night. Raghu spent the next week at Delhi being indoctrinated into the department's ethos. The appointment letters for him and Kalpana had been issued by Maninder the morning after their meeting.

By the time Raghu reached Kerala, the news had spread. A large contingent of tourism department officials was at the airport to receive him. Santhamma, the deputy director was also there. Santhamma had done her schooling at Switzerland, where her father had worked in a multinational firm. After her training in tourism and hospitality in France, she had returned to Kerala. She had met Raghu when she come down to the government house and had once complemented him on the efficient running of the estate. There was a reversal of roles now. Raghu had become her boss.

Santhamma did not mind. She was sure that they would make a great team. With Maninder's blessing they would rejuvenate Kerala tourism. She looked forward to starting work.

Raghu and Kalpana moved to a new government bungalow at Trivandrum, the state capitol. Their place was close to Raghu's new office. There was a string of tourist bungalows and other government assets all over the state which were being underutilized or misused. They had reluctantly handed over charge of the government house at Kottayam to a recently recruited young officer. His name was Dilip. Raghu was impressed by Dilip's knowledge of computers and by his capability for hard work. He was humble and well mannered. Dilip was also a master of the Kerala martial art Kalarippayattu.

Kalpana's office also was at Trivandrum. The tourism department ran a string of boutiques all over the country. They financed handicraft industries and gave loans to craftsmen.

Maninder had suggested that the two of them study the working of their departments from within for a month. They could then attempt a much needed revamp. Dilip had done an excellent job at the Kottayam guest house. He had streamlined the running of the various sub-departments and also merged the government house to the tourist map. There were always a couple of international tourists staying on the premises. Raghu gave Dilip charge of the Kottayam zone. This included three more tourist bungalows in extreme states of disrepair. Dilip was only too happy to accept the challenge.

Chapter 5   The Tourism Department gets a New Look

Santhamma and Raghu sat and worked out schemes for revamping the department, while generating funds through innovative tourism. Kettuvalloms or Kerala houseboats were making a comeback. Eco-tourism in the hills was poised to take off. They entered into an understanding with 'ecolinks', the international pioneers of ecotourism. If they could keep the industry clean and fair, Kerala could become a major tourist destination and hub. The private sector was heavily into the tourist boom. But only a small segment of the industry was organized and a select few maintained acceptable standards. The rest were 'fly by night' operators, interested only in making a fast buck. They cut on quality and costs and fleeced the tourists whenever they could. Tourism was built on reputations. If supervision was not exercised, mainstream tourism would remain a trickle.

With Dilip's help they linked up the Kerala tourist website to the international travel agencies. Tourism packages were revamped and reintroduced. The packages were comprehensive and included air tickets, accommodation and various options for transport and cuisine. The new packages became popular very soon. Raghu would personally visit the hotels and houseboats to ensure that requisite standards were being maintained. But trouble was brewing. Local con men and a few small operators were getting elbowed out. They united under a political group.

When Raghu visited Alleppy, he was greeted with red flags. Hired goons went on a rampage. One of the houseboats was burnt. Tourists were heckled and one Israeli lady molested. The opposition party newspaper screamed that our culture was being sold. Someone burnt an American flag and an effigy of George Bush. The flow of tourists dwindled to a trickle.

 Raghu contacted Maninder for help. But Maninder was having his hands full. Every ministry they had tried to cleanse and rejuvenate was rebelling. The modus operandi of the middle men and profiteers was similar everywhere. Rabble rousing on grounds of caste, religion or tradition was a simple affair. Any highway project could be stalled and any defence deal scrapped if you had the capability to organize demonstrations and controlled a newspaper to carry disinformation. If Raghu had to turn around Kerala tourism, he would have to do it without Maninder's help.

Raghu was ready to give up. He realized the wisdom of previous governments who handed out directorial portfolios for political patronage. A large chunk of the money would get siphoned off, but some work could be done. Raghu was powerless. Meanwhile Kalpana had resigned her post as joint director in the handloom department. She had been sickened by the corruption and stifled by the undercurrents.

One day Raghu had a visit from Suresh Menon. Suresh Menon had been a student union leader and was Dilip's friend. He had spearheaded many student agitations and was an icon of youth idealism. He had gone to Australia for his training in business administration and had recently returned to Kerala. He had followed press reports of Raghu's tourism initiatives with great interest. The fact that the initiative had boomeranged had saddened him. Suresh knew that dynamic and sustained tourism would be an answer to many of the state's woes. It would also improve the image of his beloved Kerala.

Raghu, Santha and Dilip had a meeting with Suresh. Raghu explained his tourism initiative to the youth leader. The tourism package deals were the first phase. With the money that came in, there would be a major restoration of the government tourist bungalows to world standards. With the memoranda of understanding they had with the various nature and tourism organizations Kerala would have been a top tourist destination soon. But the agitation and violence had thrown a spanner in the works. International tourism organizations wanted peace and stability. Once that was denied, they withdrew. Raghu planned to resign soon.

Suresh was certain that the project could be revived. A born leader, he was sure that he could make the populace see reason. Tourism was the future for many of Kerala's townships. By bowing to the profiteers, we were doing the state a grave injustice. Suresh Menon was a big name in Kerala politics. No political party would take him on casually. He contacted the local leaders and got them to back off from the agitation. Once the local toughs realized that Suresh was involved, they opted to join in with Raghu's plans rather than risk being isolated. A new set of package tourism deals was announced. The show hit the road again.

Kalpana had been helping Raghu in the tourism project. She was disappointed that she had been unable to make an impact in the handicraft department and was trying to make amends. She visited the tourism department bungalows which were coming up, inculcating traditional architectural and décor into the constructions. Meanwhile, the handicrafts department was in absolute shambles. It was just a ruse to siphon away government money in the name of culture.

The department of Tourism was doing well. The department acquired a whole fleet of Kettuvalloms, with all the modern amenities including electronic connectivity. Restoration work was on in the resorts. They now offered traditional herbal cures and massages and even initiation into the art of Kalarippayattu.

Elections were drawing near again. The state assembly elections of Kerala would be held at the same time. Maninder's party was facing difficulties. The opposition had succeeded in polarizing the electorate on caste and communal lines. There were riots and communal disturbances all over the country. Despite all the economic gains and prosperity, the election could go either way. Suresh had become more active in Kerala politics. He was being widely spoken of as the next chief minister of the state.

Chapter 6   The Children Grow Up

Raghu had never taken an active interest in politics. His son Sumant surprised him. After completing his schooling, he had come back to Kerala and had joined the Government Arts College, which was a hotbed of youth politics in the state. His younger brother Hemant joined the National Defence Academy at Pune. Hemant had always been good at sports and he excelled at the academy. He was an expert horseman and did fairly well in his academics. If he were lucky he could even win the academies' sword of honour.

Maninder's party scraped back into power through a coalition ministry. A number of small regional parties with no national agenda except avarice and greed had to be coopted to achieve a majority. Suresh's party lost the state elections but was part of the ruling coalition at the centre.

Hemant passed out from the academy with distinction. He missed the sword of honour by a whisker. Despite much cajoling from Kalpana, he opted for the infantry and was posted to the Gorkha regiment. His unit would be taking up position at the Siachen glazier during his first appointment. The family had a get together at Kerala before his departure. Raghu, Kalpana and the two brothers spend a week at the wild life resort at Thekkady. The place had been transformed from the time of their childhood visit. There were nature trails and tree houses. Elephants ferried tourists on jungle safaris. A few islands in the lake were out of bounds for regular tourists. Rare and endangered species thrived in these hamlets, away from their natural predators and the probing cameras of tourists.

In the evenings, the family would sit around the verandah, protected from mosquitoes by an almost invisible net. They discussed values and perceptions and individual plans. Hemant was an idealist. "The hot blood of patriotism flows richly through his veins", thought Raghu proudly. Sumant was pragmatic. His foray into the field of politics had made him worldly wise. "Pure idealism was fruitless", Sumant reiterated. A certain degree of shrewdness was required for an individual to be effective. Raghu tended to agree with Sumant. His roller coaster ride as the director of tourism had taught him many valuable lessons. They talked about Suresh Menon. Sumant was a great fan of his and they shared a great bonhomie despite being on opposite sides of the political fence. Hemant had always been and would remain Kalpana's pet. The fact that he was now going to be an infantry officer was a constant source of anxiety for her. The holiday was over all too soon.

Maninder had expanded Raghu's zone of control. He was now heading the national tourism board. He tried to replicate his Kerala experiment in other parts of the country. To some extend he succeeded. He was however often stymied in his efforts by local politicians and their vested interests. Maninder could not openly support him in many ventures. He had to keep the coalition government functional. Kalpana had her hands full, helping Raghu in his plans. On Raghu's recommendation, Dilip had been given charge of the handicrafts department. It was a skeleton department when he took over, picked clean by the political vultures of the capital. He managed to get a grip over things and take stock of the few assets that remained viable. Interacting closely with Santhamma and Raghu he set into motion an ambitious plan for the department's restoration. Santhamma and he had become friendly during his tourism days. Soon they were inseparable.

Kalpana was busy looking for suitable daughters in law for herself. She looked forward to having a couple of girls in the house she could share her joys and sorrows with.

After completing his graduation, Sumant did an MBA. He then borrowed money from a nationalized bank and set up a fisheries unit. He was a smart businessman and had repaid his loans within a year. However, politics was his first love. He would move into full time politics at an opportune time. He hoped to marry by then, so that he could transfer his businesses to his wife's name. Then there was a wedding proposal for him.

Sankaran Kutty was the icon of the Kerala Fisheries industry. He had started out with a small fleet of three boats. Today, he controlled most of the fishing off the Kerala coast. Sankaran also had interests in the timber and in the hospitality business. He made the trade name of 'Celestra', a household one, in many countries of the world. The name was a merger of his wife's name, Celin and his daughter's name Sitara. Sankaran Kutty contacted Kalpana through a common friend. Sitara would be a good match for Sumant. The wedding plans went ahead with great aplomb.

Hemant had written to Kalpana about Supriya. Supriya was a medical doctor. He had met her in his academy days at Pune, where she had been doing her medical education. Kalpana wrote off a letter to Supriya. Could she come down and meet the rest of the family. Maybe they could have a double wedding. Supriya flew down to Trivandrum to meet

Raghu and Kalpana. She brought her sister Rekha along with her. Hemant could not come down as there was some tension along the border and the unit could not spare the young officer. Supriya was a charming girl. Kalpana was quite enthralled by the young girl's wit and her demenour.

They had dinner at the press club lawns. Suresh was one of the guests. Everything went off smoothly. It seemed that the double wedding would materialize. They would plan to have the ceremonies the next year, during the Onam festival season.

Chapter 7   Terror Strikes

Christmas was drawing near. The holiday season always meant that there would be a surge of tourist activity. The Kettuvalloms were fully booked. The wild life reserve at Thekkady was packed to capacity. Even unrelated businesses thrived with the influx of tourism money. The day after Christmas, tragedy struck. Raghu was still in his office at eight in the evening when he heard the news. There had been a major terrorist attack at Alleppy.

Raghu jumped into his car and was at Alleppy almost within the hour. From a distance he could see the rich plumes of smoke from the tourist port impudently flicking its tongue at the night sky. The sound of automatic gunfire could be heard from across the lake. Raghu tried to contact the government resort manager on his cell phone. There was no reply to the ring tune. The road was blocked with traffic. There was an exodus of sorts, with everyone seemingly trying to get out of the besieged town. Raghu's car and a police jeep seemed to be the only two vehicles headed into town. The police officer in the jeep recognized Raghu. Raghu got into the police jeep with the officer after leaving his car by the roadside. Then, lights flashing, they went on to the tourist resort. The officer told him what had happened.

Soon after sunset, three speedboats were seen cruising towards the tourist boat berths. The Kettuvalloms were mostly out on the lake with their tourists. Two of the boats had docked near the resort. Masked men from the boats had charged into the resort lobbing grenades and firing automatic weapons. The police force responded late. By the time they reached the site the terrorists had retreated to their boats.

Kerala policemen were too poorly trained and inadequately armed to tackle terrorists with automatic weapons. Meanwhile the speed boats were out on the lake, attacking the kettuvalloms. The one patrol boat that the police owned, was under repair. There were private boat owners. All of them refused to take their boats out. Courage and community sense were rare commodities in this part of the country.

The police jeep reached the resort. The buildings were on fire. There were groups of tourists huddled together on the lawns. Raghu was appalled to see that the wounded had yet not been shifted to hospital. The houses around the resort were all deserted. Once the attack occurred, the locals had locked their houses and fled. No one wanted to be involved. Raghu rang up the district hospital using his mobile telephone. They did not have ambulances and they were unsure if they could manage a large number of casualties.

Raghu felt a tap on his shoulder. It was Dilip. Suresh, Dilip and Santhamma had come down in Suresh's car as soon as they heard of the attack. Suresh was already taking charge. Santhamma was busy supervising the first aid. They did some quick assessment. There were at least a hundred people who needed urgent medical attention. Scattered bursts of gunfire from across the water suggested that terrorists were still hunting down the Kettuvalloms. One of the tourists at the resort was an ex marine. As soon as the attack at the resort occurred, he had contacted his friend who was out on one of the houseboats. A message was passed to all the houseboat crews, to douse their lights and head for the nearest shore. The houseboats were too slow to make fast getaways. With their lights out however, they would be more difficult for the terrorists to hunt down.

Suresh had driven to the district medical college. He came back driving a bus. There were ten young doctors with him. He had picked them up from the resident doctor's quarters. The rest of the doctors in the hostel had rushed to the hospital to get things ready. They would soon receive mass casualties. They broke open the dispensary and collected all the emergency medical supplies that would be needed.

The youngsters trusted and adored Suresh. He would back them up if the administration acted funny.

Dilip had located the resort's speed boat. Philip was with him. They managed to start up the speed boat's engines. Dilip rummaged around the boat house looking for weapons they could use against the terrorists. Inside a locker he found a scuba knife and a harpoon gun. There were also a couple of fishing nets. With their lights doused they headed out into the lake. The terrorists were in for a surprise. The hunters would now become the hunted.

Raghu had got some help to sift through the rubble. There was a National Cadet Corps camp at the nearby college. Hearing of the attack, they had rushed to the scene. Soon around fifty young and eager young men and women had reached the resort. There were still many victims trapped within the building. A full-scale rescue effort was soon on. The casualties were evacuated to the hospital in the commandeered bus. The hospital operation theatres were soon running. The resident doctors were at their motivated best. Nursing students from the nearby school had also poured in. Suresh established a communication centre. From his laptop he posted information about the casualties on the tourism department web site. Concerned relatives of the tourists from all over logged on to get information on their loved ones.

Raghu knew the flight commander from the Naval Base. Captain Khan had stayed at the resort with his family earlier. Raghu had had dinner with them on one of his inspection visits. Khan had heard of the attack. A formal request for assistance would need to be made by the state administration. Meanwhile there was a night flying training sortie already scheduled. Khan would divert it over the lake and would be in the helicopter himself. Dilip and Philip had identified one of the terrorist speed boats. Ahead they could make out the silhouette of a houseboat with its lights doused. The houseboat was trying to make to the shore. There was a stutter of automatic gunfire from the terrorist boat followed by a small explosion on board the houseboat as their fuel tank exploded. The terrorists were closing in for a kill.

Dilip's boat had not been seen by the terrorists. Philip cut engines as they glided in. The terrorists were probably considering taking hostages. There were four men in the terrorist boat and their attention was focused on the house boat. There was a hiss of compressed air as Philip fired the harpoon. The man at the controls slumped forward, the harpoon transfixing his neck to the wooden wheel. The boat had spun out of control, hurling the three remaining terrorists to the floor. This was the break they needed. Dilip jumped on to terrorist boat, his scuba knife plunging into another terrorist's neck. Philip had reloaded the harpoon gun and the second terrorist who whirled on Dilip froze as a harpoon punctured his chest. Philip also jumped on the boat. It was over in a trice. The four terrorists were dead. A radio was stuttering in the terrorist's boat. Philip pointed to the horizon. Another terrorist boat was headed for them.

Their own boat had drifted quite a distance away and the second terrorist boat would be upon them before they could swim to it. Picking up the automatic weapons from the fallen terrorists, they slipped over the edge of the boat and lay in the water holding their weapons above the water level. They could not see the approaching boat but could hear its throbbing engines. There was silence as the approaching boat engines were switched off. Dilip and Philip heard curses. The dead terrorists had been seen. There was a burst of gunfire as the terrorists fired at the Kettuvallom. They were under the impression that the opposition was in the houseboat. Philip and Dilip peeked over the boats side. The approaching boat was only about ten yards away. Three terrorists were crouched, pointing their automatic weapons at the houseboat. Easing their automatic weapons over the boats edge, they fired together. In two short bursts of fire, they downed the three terrorists. The fourth was whirling the boat around trying to get away, when the petrol tank caught fire. There were flames all around him now, and his clothes were burning. He managed to get the burning boat a good hundred yards away. Then it exploded.

Captain Khan saw the explosion from his helicopter as he headed out over the lake. Then he spotted another speed boat making for the open sea. He realized at once, that some terrorists were making a getaway. He changed course to give chase. A fusillade of bullets from the fleeing boat smashed into the helicopter's canopy. He was flying a reconnaissance chopper not meant for this kind of combat. He urged his helicopter into a steep climb. Captain Khan was carrying depth charges. Hovering above the speeding boat at a relatively safe distance he released the charges. A plume of water seemed to engulf the speed boat. When it settled, the boat was nowhere to be seen. The battle was over. His fuel was running low. Khan realized that a bullet must have punctured one of the fuel tanks. He headed back to base. Dilip and Philip swam to the house boat. Surprisingly no one inside had been hurt. They had seen the last terrorist speed boat getting blown out of the water by the helicopter's depth charge. They retrieved their drifting boat.

Philip used the houseboats radio to wire the others. It was safe to put on lights and head back to the tourist berth. Three houseboats had been sunk. The occupants had been herded to another boat where they had been tied up. A naval patrol boat reached the boat and rescued the prisoners. The terrorists had planned to take them hostage.

Dilip and Philips were not finished with the operation. They had learned from Raghu that the last boat had been attempting to flee to the open sea. Surely there was a ship waiting to receive them. Dilip and Philip headed out to the shipping channel. Just outside the harbour, there were ships waiting for harbour entry. Most were cargo carriers. Philip noted down their identification. The rest would be a job for Interpol. They had almost turned back when they saw a midsized vessel making its way to the harbour mouth. Dilip turned the boat around and headed to investigate. It was likely that the crew would have seen any ship which was headed out in a hurry. As they drew nearer, Dilip's heart skipped a beat. The ship was a fishing assistance vessel belonging to Sankaran. It s name was clear in the approaching boats lights. It was the Celeste 1. They could get all the help they needed. The Celeste 1 carried al the latest tracking technology and speed boats. They should be able to locate and track down any vessel in the area. Dilip called up Raghu.

Sankaran would have to be contacted. Raghu would take care of that. By the time they drew alongside, Sankaran had already issued instructions to the ship's captain. A ladder was lowered. Two well-built sailors got down into the boat as Dilip and Raghavan climbed on board. The ship had a special hatch which could be opened to take in smaller boats while at sea. The sailors would do the necessary. Dilip briefed Xavier, the ship's captain on all that had happened and of their plan to trace the terrorist's 'mother ship'.

Xavier had been instructed by Sankaran to extend all possible cooperation. They turned the ship around in a wider part of the channel and headed out. They had switched on their tracking systems and soon every ship in a hundred mile radius could be seen on screen. They could afford to ignore the smaller blips which probably belonged to fishing boats. The ships moving towards the harbour could also probably be excluded.

There were two medium sized vessels which were heading north-west. The Celeste gave chase. They caught up with the first vessel in the early hours of the morning. The 'Monte Carlo' was a Spanish vessel with a crew of mixed nationality. Xavier raised the ship's captain on his radio. He explained the situation and requested permission for Dilip and Philip to come on board, to ask a few questions to the crew. There was a pause. Xavier guessed that the captain would be checking the Celeste 1's antecedents from his data bank. Pirates were not very common in the Arabian Sea. It was prudent to be cautious. Soon the Captain came on line again. A clearance was given.

A small motor boat was launched. Dilip and Philip were lowered into the motorboat and taken to the 'Monte Carlo'. They climbed a rope ladder to reach the deck. The crewmen were cordial. They had not seen any suspicious vessels in the locality. The two of them were given a walking tour of the ship. She was carrying iron ore. There was nothing suspicious on board. After thanking the captain profusely, they returned to the Celeste. The other vessel had meanwhile changed course. They now seemed to be heading due west. Celeste followed her course. Dilip decided to ask for assistance from the coast guard. The vessel they were pursuing was moving too fast and too erratically to be a bona fide cargo vessel. If they were indeed a terrorist vessel, it was unlikely that they would stop for the Celeste.

They checked out the Celeste's armoury. The Celeste was surprisingly well equipped. There was an array of guns and assorted depth charges. They had automatic weapons and even a small machine gun for antipiracy deterrence. To stop and board a hostile armed vessel in the high seas however, would require higher grade weaponry.

The coast guard responded quickly. A Dornier aircraft had already located the vessel and instructed the fleeing ship to stop engines. The ship, which had by now been identified as the 'Viking' was ignoring orders and trying to make a run for it. A fast interceptor craft of the coast guard caught up with the 'Viking' by mid noon. A warning shot across her bows from the interceptor gave the Viking's captain no options. He stopped engines. The Celeste was also now within range. With the Dornier circling overhead an armed boarding party from the coast guard vessel stormed the ship. There was no resistance. The Celeste had also drawn alongside by then. Dilip and Philip also got on board. The crew had been lined up at gunpoint on the deck. They were a motley lot. The coast guard was searching the ship. They found crates of illicit drugs, crudely packed in wooden crates and barrels. There were very few weapons on board. The Viking was smuggling drugs. This was not the terrorist vessel. Leaving the coast guard to tackle the smugglers, Philip and Dilip returned to the Celeste. The terrorist vessel had apparently disappeared into thin air. They returned to Alleppy.

There had been other arracks at Goa and in Rajasthan. The casualties had been higher there. It would be a while before the average tourist ventured into India again. The modus operandi of the attacks had been different in each instance. The timing and the common theme suggested a matrix of terror controlled by one mastermind or organization. The synchronised and organised attacks with no financial motives suggested sponsorship by an international organisation with state support. There was pressure on Maninder's government to retaliate. Maninder was wary.

It was against international law to launch attacks against the socalled terrorist camps in another nation's territory. Terrorist casualties would be few and it could trigger off war which would result in more deaths. Tension across the border was however unavoidable. There were isolated skirmishes and incidents of 'hot pursuit' of mercenaries across the border. Hemant's unit was in the thick of things. Kalpana was beside herself with anxiety.

Chapter 8 Wedding Time

Then Kalpana's fears came true. There had been no news from Hemant for a fortnight. Then a call came. It was Hemant. He was calling from the Army hospital at Delhi. His right foot had been injured by an exploding anti personal mine. He had been evacuated to a field hospital and then flown to Delhi. The surgeons who operated on his leg told him that there was a fifty percent chance of saving his leg. They were trying their best but the blood supply to the foot was precarious.

Kalpana and Raghu took the next flight to Delhi. Hemant was out of intensive care and in the ward. He seemed cheerful enough. The infection soon came under control. Within a week the surgeon grew more optimistic. If all went well, Hemant should be walking in a couple of months. Supriya was there by Hemant's side, when they reached. She had been hearing of the border skirmishes and was grateful that Hemant had got off so easily. At least he was alive.

It was three months before Hemant was discharged from the hospital. His foot had been saved, but his ankle was severely damaged. He would never be able to run or jump normally. His soldiering days were over. When he went home on sick leave, the family sat around and discussed his future. If he stayed on in the army, he would be relegated to a desk job. It would be better if he opted out. He was still young and could make himself a career. Sulekha had come down with Hemant. Kalpana got busy planning her son's wedding. The double wedding would go as scheduled.

Tourism was slowly picking up again. Terrorism was a universal phenomenon. In a month the tourists started trickling back. The resort had been rebuilt. A professional security unit was created for tourist security. Terrorism was not easy to tackle. The best they could do was to make the terrorist's job more difficult.

Sumant sold off his fisheries company and had joined Sankaran Kutty's organization. As the future son in law and heir apparent, he was in the inner circle. He continued his political activities with renewed vigour. Suresh Menon and Sumant however, seemed to have fallen out. Suresh was wary of Sankarankutty. He was convinced that Sankaran would use Sumant as a pawn. With Sankaran's financial clout and connections he could ensure that Sumant would win the coming elections. But would Sumant be able to hold his own after that. Suresh doubted it.

The wedding was a grand affair. Maninder flew down for the occasion. Sumant with Sitara and Hemant with Supriya made two very elegant couples. The evening reception had been organized by Sankaran Kutty at a five-star hotel at Trivandrum. Maninder however, could not attend the reception as he had some previous commitments. The next morning, the couples left for a whirlwind honeymoon in Europe. They were back in a fortnight. Sumant had to get back to his company and Hemant's management course in Australia would be starting soon.

Sankaran Kutty had constructed a penthouse apartment for his daughter and son in law, overlooking the Cochin harbour. Supriya opted to stay with Kalpana and Raghu at Trivandrum. There was a centre of excellence of cardiac surgery at Trivandrum close to their place. She wished to train in cardiac anaesthesia there. It would keep her busy while Hemant pursued his management studies.

The elections drew near. Sankarankutty was sparing no effort, fair or foul to ensure that his son in law would win. Sumant was a likely candidate for chief minister. Maninder's party had stepped down from power, as they could no longer accede to the demands of the coalition. Once again central elections and the elections to the Kerala state assembly would be together.

Hemant was doing well at his university. He scored excellent grades in his preliminary examinations and could pick the courses of his choice. He decided to shift to law. Supriya was expecting a baby. She was enjoying her apprenticeship in cardiac surgery. Kalpana was exceptionally fond of this daughter in law. She effectively handed over all the household decision making to Supriya. Sitara and Sumant were busy with their lives. They rarely visited Sumant's parents.

Chapter 9   Raghu Resigns

The elections were over. Maninder's party had suffered an abject humiliation. Maninder himself had barely scraped through. He was half tempted to forgo politics altogether. His party had however been battered in the elections and would need restructuring. Maninder could not desert his party men in this hour of need.

In Kerala, Sumant's party came to power after engineering a few defections and wooing the few independent candidates. Sumant became the youngest chief minister in Kerala's history. Raghu soon resigned his directorship of the tourism department. He was offered an executive post in a multinational company, but he declined. He would accept a few consultancies and lecture requests. Raghu was not keen on accepting any regular employment.

He had brought some property near the Government house, where he had started his career. A man should be his own master at least after retirement. The house he constructed there was not ostentatious, but comfortable and well planned. In the courtyard, there were coconut and mango trees for him to tend.

There were a whole lot of books he had wanted to read, but never had the time for. Raghu was certain that he would enjoy his retired life. Kalpana had volunteered for some social activities and would keep herself occupied with women's issues. She was the founder president of the Kerala organization for preventing atrocities against women. Despite their education, the women of Kerala were always doing a delicate balancing act between keeping their masochistic husbands happy and their careers afloat.

After Raghu retired, it was expected that Santhamma would take over as the tourism director. The new government in power however had their own plans. The stooge they appointed as the chief of tourism was corrupt and inefficient. Santhamma resigned her appointment. She moved in with Dilip. Much to the chagrin of the moral brigade, they refused to get officially married.

Sumant's stint as chief minister was an apparent success. Corruption was at an all-time high, forests were being denuded. Industries who paid a political tariff could afford to ignore pollution laws with equanimity. But there was money flowing into the state and the stock market boomed. There were no paralyzing strikes. The trade union leaders got their slice of the pie. Suresh had to admit that the government seemed to be functioning. It was relatively quiet at the border now. A year of good harvests ensured that the granaries were full. Dilip continued as the director of the handicraft's ministry. His sheer dynamism ensured his continuation in spite of political changes.

Chapter 10   Watchdog International.

Hemant finished his law school in the top ten of his class. He could have chosen any appointment he wanted. He surprised everyone by joining the relatively underpaid organization called watchdog international. The organization was based in Geneva. This organization monitored corrupt practices, human rights abuse and terrorist activities all over the world.

Hemant was given charge of a section which dealt with terrorist funds. He was quite shocked at the amount of money that was diverted to terrorist and subversive organizations all over the world. The money came from drugs, gun running and extortion. In return, the terrorists offered protection to the drug runners and shared information and resources with the crime lords. It was a mutually beneficial and sustaining nexus.

Supriya was now a cardiac anaesthesiologist. She had moved to Geneva with Hemant and had got her European Union certification. Their son Sheshank was four years old and attended play-school. Hemant and Sumant communicated very little. They had initially made it a point to meet once a year at

Kerala. Kalpana and Supriya were very fond of each other. It was a different equation between Kalpana and Sitara. The tension between the two of them was almost palpable. They rarely visited each other.

Suresh was busy in his political affairs. It was widely known that he was the decision maker of the Celesta group now. Sitara was officially the chairperson of the board. Sankaran Kutty was staying out of the limelight. Sitara and Sumant did not have any children.

Hemant was busy in his terrorist money investigations. There were rumours of large influxes of terrorist money into India. Hemant also had access to a list of Indian politicians who had money stashed away in secret bank accounts. The list included a large number or prominent public figures of Indian politics. He was glad to note that Maninder's name was not in the list.

The terror money that reached India was being processed through one large organization which had been code named the octopus. The identity of the organization had not been discovered despite the best efforts of Interpol. Hemant made it his mission to discover the identity of the octopus. He was not a field operative. He would need to establish a field cell in India. Watchdog international would bear the expenses.

It was vacation time. Hemant and Supriya, along with their son Sheshank decided to visit Kerala. They met Sumant and Sitara at their official residence at Trivandrum. The two of them were busy with a trade delegation which had come to Kerala. They could spend only a few minutes with Hemant and his family. Hemant, Supriya and Sheshank went on to Kottayam in Raghu's car.

Hemant had seen the house come up but the garden was a present surprise. The mango trees were in full bloom. There were pineapples and mulberries in the garden. Raghu had green fingers which had been crying for use after his government house days. He was now finding fulfilment in his rediscovered vocation.

That evening Raghu and Hemant sat out in the lawns and talked while Supriya and Kalpana lead Sheshank on an exploration of the garden which he described as his tropical jungle. Raghu had gifted him a butterfly net and he ran around the garden after those nimble beauties. Hemant told Raghu about the terror money being funnelled into India and about the elusive organization called the octopus. He spoke of his plan to set up an investigative cell to unveil the identity of this enigma.

Raghu was concerned. Hemant was still the idealist he had been in the army. This type of investigation involved significant risk and could invite retaliation. With his internationally recognized law degree, Hemant could pick a job of his choice. Could he not find something more peaceful?

Raghu soon realized that Hemant was totally committed to what he was doing. He suggested that Hemant should tie up something with Suresh Menon. Suresh was now staying out of active politics. He was running a non-Governmental organization for the prevention of tribal exploitation. Kalpana had worked with him on many projects involving tribal women.

 Sheshank and the ladies were back from the garden. They all gathered round the kitchen helping to get dinner ready. Kalpana did not have any 'live-in' help. A maid came in once a day to mop, sweep and cut vegetables. They managed the rest of the chores by themselves.

The next morning Hemant took Raghu's van and drove to Suresh's NGO. The headquarters of the organization was situated in the hills. There was no telephone or electricity there. Here, Suresh ran a vocational training course for the tribals. Hemant found the view enticing and the roads challenging. It was a long and winding road through the rubber plantations. The scenery was so beautiful that he wished he had brought Supriya and Sheshank with him. Raghu however had offered to take the family fishing to the Meenachil River which was just down the hill. They owned a small ancestral plot with a grove of coconut trees by the river's edge. It would be a picnic for Sheshank. The ladies had been busy in the morning packing a picnic lunch. Hemant wondered if they had caught any fish yet.

He stopped the van at a roadside teashop to ask for directions. There was a mud tack ten kilometers ahead. One hours drive uphill from there and he would reach the tribal colony. He was grateful for the van's four-wheel drive. The mud-track was treacherous and the road steep. After grunting and groaning uphill for what seemed like eternity, the van reached a rickety rusted iron gate. He opened the gate and drove on in. Ahead of him was a clearing in the forest. There were huts all around the periphery and in the centre was a long shed. The forest around was dense and thick. Behind the settlement was a high mountain. Clouds around the top hid the cliff's peak. As his van drew up alongside the shed, Suresh stepped out of the shed. Hemant had been unable to warn Suresh of his trip. Suresh was astonished and genuinely pleased to see who his visitor was. Suresh escorted Hemant around the colony. As they walked around, he explained the working of his organization.

For centuries the tribal men and women had been exploited by landowners, traders and politicians. Suresh's organization aimed at making them self-reliant. They went round the tribal settlements selecting men and women with leadership potential. At the colony they were made literate and given a crash course in relevant law and tribal rights. They were taught a few engineering skills for water harvesting and distribution and tutored in basic carpentry. After a year, these tribals would return to their settlements to attempt to make a change. Some of the recruits were successful. Some however disappeared with their skills to the metropolis to make a good living for themselves. A thorny issue was the animosity between tribes. The Tulsi tribals were sworn enemies of the Tuttus and refused to attend any training camps where Tuttus were present. Hemant was surprised as to how Suresh had aged. His flowing beard and sparse hair made him look more like a Christian missionary than like a retired chief minister.

It was lunch time and Hemant joined Suresh and the tribals at communal lunch. As they sat on coir mats eating rice and curry off freshly cut banana leaves, Hemant told Suresh of his mission. Suresh looked sharply at Hemant. The nexus of crime ran very deep and the men involved were dangerous. Suresh would agree to do the field work, if Hemant promised to act upon the findings. Hemant assured him that his organization was dead serious.

There would be expenses involved. It would be imprudent to pay the money directly to Suresh. A figurehead organization would be required to route the funds. Suresh suggested that they contact Dilip. The handicrafts department had plenty of overseas dealings and would provide an ideal cover. Suresh agreed to accompany Hemant to Kottayam. Raghu and Kalpana would have a surprise guest. They drove back to Kottayam in the van.

It had been a long time since Suresh had come to their house. Raghu embraced him warmly. The two of them settled down to sip some sweet toddy Raghu ordered from a nearby shop. Sheshank proudly showed them the fish he had caught. He had refused to let his mother clean and cook it earlier. After they all had a group photograph with the fish, he handed the trophy to his mother. She could prepare it for dinner. Once more, Suresh and Raghu tried to talk Hemant out of his investigation. In the background Supriya sighed. They had been over all this before. She knew that Hemant would not budge.

The next morning Hemant and Suresh set out for Trivandrum. Raghu dropped them off at the railway station. The train journey would take around four hours. Hemant showed Suresh the list of corrupt Indian politicians with illicit money stashed abroad. Suresh chuckled as he went through the list.

They had informed Dilip that they would be coming. Dilip's car and chauffer were at the station to receive them. Dilip was at an important meeting that would get over only by three in the afternoon. Santhamma was out of town. She had gone to Kochi to visit a sick relative. After his meeting was over Dilip drove the three of them down to a beach hotel that belonged to his department. They had a late lunch and over lunch they exchanged pleasantries.

Lunch was over. Hemant broached the topic of their visit. He explained the working of 'Watchdog International' and of the trail of terror money that lead to India. He told them all he knew of the elusive octopus, which was precious little. He explained his plan to set up an investigative field cell in India. His organization would provide all the necessary funding. They could involve the Interpol once they had evidence of some kind. Once the octopus was identified, they could leave the rest to watchdog international. Dilip thought for a while. There was no problem. In a week, he would set up a department of tribal handicrafts to which both Suresh and Hemant could have access. The department would be under his direct supervision and the transactions would come to no one's notice but his.

 It was time for Suresh and Hemant to return to Kottayam. Dilip had some work at Kochi. He had been planning to drive down anyway and he could bring Santhamma back with him. He would take a small diversion and drop off Suresh and Hemant at Raghu's place.

It was almost midnight when they reached Kottayam. Kalpana had picked up the phone when they rang up from Trivandrum to say that they would be coming late by car. She had insisted that they have dinner at home, however late they were. Sheshank was fast asleep. The rest of them ate rice and fish curry before retiring for the night. Early the next morning, Dilip continued on to Kochi. Hemant and Suresh would drive on to Suresh's camp later in the day. Sheshank and Supriya would go with them.

The drive through the mountain mud path was a new experience for Sheshank. Suresh told them that at times elephants would be seen crossing the path. If that happened, they would just have to kill the engines and wait. Unfortunately, they saw no elephants. Hemant and his family planned to spend the night at the camp. A tent was rigged up for them replete with mosquito nets. They all had dinner around a camp fire. Then the family retired to their tent.

One of the tribal hunters took Sheshank on a small hunt in the morning. They went out early in the morning armed with bows and arrows and returned an hour later with two dead rabbits in their bag. The rabbits were dumped into a sack and put in the van's boot. Sheshank would have something special for dinner tonight. They spend their last two days in Kerala at home. Then they flew back to Geneva.

In a week, the tribal handicrafts centre had been set up. Dilip drove his official jeep down to meet Suresh. They chalked out a plan of action together. Suresh was to make a press statement that he was researching material for a book. It would trace the history of the city over two centuries and would culminate in the terrorist attacks on tourist resorts attacks at Alleppy that had occurred almost a decade ago. This would give them an illusionary cover to restart the investigation. The police department's investigation had spluttered to a close a year ago without a single definitive lead.

Chapter 11   The Investigation Gathers Steam

Suresh started his investigation. Meanwhile Hemant transferred money to the tribal handicrafts account for contingencies. Dilip contacted Philip who had been with him that fateful night. Philip was settled at Florida where he ran a sailing school. He also had a dog training centre where they bred and trained dogs for the police forces. Dilip told him of Hemant's investigation. Philip was game. He agreed to fly down to India and join Suresh's group. He flew down to India and was picked up by Suresh from the airport. He had brought with him Stephan, a German shepherd that he was training.

The team recreated the attack bit by bit. They traced the occupants of the tourist bungalow that night from the departmental records. One by one, the witnesses were interviewed again. Suresh was amazed at the amount of fresh information they could gather. The witnesses had been in a state of shock when they had been interviewed by the police after the attack. Now they could recapitulate everything in detail. They had a clearer picture now. There had been 12 men involved in the attack; all of them were brown skinned. At least two of them spoke with a south Indian accent. Only six bodies had been recovered and none of the bodies had been identified.

They held a summit meet at Suresh's camp. Dilip came up with a suggestion. The young men had to have come from somewhere. They must have been reported as missing or dead. They hired a group to sift through all the obituaries of young men reported as missing or dead during that period. They drew a blank. There were no cases on record where a group of young men had disappeared and the bodies had not been found.

It was Dilip who noted a news item that solved the mystery. A fishing boat had been lost in a freak storm off the coast of Chennai around that time. Six of the crew men had been reported missing. Their bodies had not been found. They traced the records of the missing fishing boat from the port records. The fishing boat Tarangini was reported to have been lost with a crew of six. What was unusual was that there was no report of bad weather in any of the meteorological reports at that time. They got a shock when they identified the owner of the boat. The boat belonged to the Celeste fishing flotilla. The crew men were a mystery. There were no leads there. The list of names of the crew lost had been removed from the records.

Dilip and Philip remembered the Celeste 1, the sophisticated and armed fishing support vessel that they had found at the harbour mouth after the terror attack. Could she have been waiting for the terrorist boats to return after their strike? They grimaced when they remembered how they had contacted the ship for assistance. They had even managed to capture a band of smugglers who had been unfortunate enough to have been around at that time.

It was indeed a brilliant ploy by the mastermind of the attack. A lost boat could explain away the missing men to their families. In the high seas neither the bodies nor the boat would be expected to be found. Philips had a brain wave. What, if the boat had not really been sunk? If they could trace the Tarangini, they would have their first bit of direct evidence.

They got the engine number and the specifications of Tarangini from the records. They would have to trace out the new boats registered around that time. One of these could be the Tarangini. Philips set out to investigate. There was a disappointment in store for them. None of the new boats registered around that time matched the specifications of the Tarangini. On a hunch Philips checked the records of fishing boat sales. He struck gold. The fishing boat Gracias had been bought by a Goan company.

The previous registered owner of the boat was Celeste international.

Philips paid a visit to the Goan ship yard. After two days of search he found the Gracias. She was dry docked for hull repairs. He got on board in the guise of a potential buyer. In the engine room the number on the engine did not match that of the Tarangini. At a closer look, he realized that the number had been painted over. He scraped away the paint to look beneath. He smiled to himself as the old number emerged. The Gracias was the Tarangini. Celeste had sold a fishing boat that they had reported as sunk after changing its name.

Dilip wired Hemant. There was important information that they wished to share. Decisions had to be made. Hemant guessed that the team must have got close to the Octopus. The same night he was on a flight to India.

Chapter 12   Hostage

Supriya was getting ready for hospital the next morning, when she received an unexpected telephone call. It was Sumant. He was in Europe for a visit and would come to Geneva later in the day. Sitara had sent some gifts for Sheshank. Supriya was pleasantly surprised at this sudden affection. Unfortunately, she had major cardiac surgery scheduled for the day. She would not be free. She gave Sumant the address of Sheshank's play school. She would inform the caretaker there to expect Sheshank's uncle from India. As Sumant was leaving the same afternoon, she would be unable to meet him.

The day was a busy one for Supriya. The old man undergoing the open-heart procedure had been operated twice earlier. His heart muscle was flabby and would not resume its contractions once the surgery was complete. Finally, when the heart started beating again, it flew into all sorts of bizarre arrhythmias. It was late evening when she returned to the play school. She was sure that Sheshank would have been playing with his friends and would not have minded the delay.

When she reached the crèche she was in for a jolt. Sheshank's uncle had offered to take him home. As the play school had been warned about his arrival they had reluctantly agreed. They had tried to contact Supriya, but she was busy at surgery, a message had been left on her mobile. She hurried home. There was no one there. Sitting back in the car she checked her mobile. There was a long message from Hemant. She would read it later. The other message was from the Creche that Shashank's uncle was insisting that she had told him to take Sheshank home. Was it all right? Supriya went back to Hemant's message. It detailed the discoveries of Suresh and his team. She shuddered as she read that Celeste was related to the elusive 'Octopus'. Sumant would be involved. In a flash she realized that her son had been kidnapped. Disconsolate and Sobbing, she drove to the police station.

Dilip, Hemant, Suresh and Philip were huddled together finalizing the report for watchdog international when Supriya's telephone call came. As Hemant took the call, they could see his face turn an ashen white. Clutching the table for support he was reassuring her. Sheshank would not get harmed. After all, Sumant was his uncle. They could sort out issues with him. He put the phone down. He knew that his reassurance to Supriya was hollow. He sat down and appraised the others on the kidnap. They had been effectively stymied. Philip and Hemant flew to Geneva. They left Philip's dog Stephan with Raghu. Suresh would be traveling around in the next few days and Dilip would be with him.

Supriya was certain that it had been Sumant who had spoken to her on the phone. The number he had called from was registered in the name of a Mr. John Smith which was in all probability fictitious. They took some of Sumant's photographs to the playschool caretaker. She shook her head. Sumant was not the man who had picked up Sheshank. They checked with the airline. Sumant had flown out of Geneva. However, Sumant had been alone on the flight and definitely did not have a child with him. There was no evidence to link Sumant with the kidnap.

The police had already alerted a country wide search for the missing boy. Till now, there was no trace of him. Supriya suggested that they try the ports in the vicinity. Philips pointed to a fishing port on the coast of France. This was a common destination for cargo vessels from the East. They had struck pay dirt again. The Celeste had docked there a week ago to unload a consignment of frozen prawns. They had sailed out the evening of the boy's kidnap. Sheshank must be on board. It was still all conjuncture and insufficient evidence for the police to act upon. They now had to trace the Celeste themselves.

Philip had a regimental buddy who was stationed at the local NATO satellite surveillance unit. They could locate any ship in the world at any time. He would do Philip this favour. Philip and Hemant identified the Celeste for him from the satellite photographs. They finally traced her. She was two hundred kilometres off the coast of Dubai. There were scores of small fishing craft milling all around her. Philips suggested that there was a major fishing operation in progress. Philips friend corrected him. There was only one major flaw in the hypothesis. There were no large fish shoals in the area. These would have been seen on the satellite images.

There seemed to be a lot of small boats off the coast of Dubai. Philips remembered. It was the time of the great Dubai Sea Sailing Race. The race had been started a year ago to upstage the American cup. This was one of the richest races in the world. Christie, Philip's sister was a sail racing enthusiast and would be there with her boat and crew. The three of them flew down to Dubai.

Chapter 13   The Noose Tightens

Dilip received a communication from the kidnappers. The message was simple enough. If they wished to see Sheshank alive again, a set of instructions were to be followed. A compact disc had been enclosed which showed Sheshank seated facing a wooden panel. As they watched, the boy vomited. Was he unwell?

Dilip and Santhamma drove down to Raghu's place. The instructions had been explicit. Dilip was to leave Santhamma with Raghu and take Kalpana with him to Suresh Menon's camp. None of them were to leave the camp until further instructions. If any of them made any move to contact the police or to move out of their places Sheshank would be dead.

The instructions had continued. Raghu and Santhamma would receive a visitor later that evening. They were to leave the gate and the front door open and stay in the living room with the lights on. The visitor would tell them what to do. The message also warned that all of them were under constant and close surveillance and that every move was being watched.

There was a meeting going on at Sumant's penthouse. In addition to Sankarankutty and Sumant there were three others. The leader of the group was a tall man with a unkempt beard and flowing robes. The other two were Europeans dressed in their suits. The tall man spoke softly. The others leaned forward, craning their necks to listen. "Hemant's group was closing in on the octopus", the bearded Arab was saying. But as long as Sheshank remained in captivity, the octopus was safe. Dilip, Suresh and Kalpana were ensconced in the mountain camp. At a word from Shankaran Kutty, they would be eliminated. It would be made to look like a tribal uprising.

Raghu and Santhamma would be made to sign the confession that they had masterminded the tourist resort attacks. All the necessary documents had been doctored to support the claim. It would seem plausible enough. The two of them had all the inside information on the resorts. It would also explain how they had managed to reach the site of the attack so quickly. It was also suggested through the papers that the two of them had been carrying on an improper relationship. Their remorse had ultimately led on to the confession. After the confessions were signed the two of them would be eliminated. This end of the operation was crucial. It would have to be executed by someone who was absolutely reliable. Sumant raised his hand. "I will do it", he said. They looked at him with admiration. This man would certainly go places. The tall man paused and then continued. Hemant, Supriya and their friend Philip were in Europe. They were temporarily under the radar screen. Efforts were on to trace them. One of the Europeans nodded his assent. All the airline and shipping offices were under surveillance. There was no way they could get a ticket to India without coming to notice. "We will then organize a hijack. My boys have been getting out of practice". The tall Arab smiled for the first time. He guaranteed that none of the three would see Kerala again.

Chapter 14   The Grand Finale.

Philip and the others had unwittingly eluded detection. They had driven out of Geneva in a car borrowed from one of Philip's friends. At Dubai, they took a cab to the sailing port where Christie and her team were housed. The first race had been abandoned as there had been a freak storm. Christie's boat was now docked for minor repairs. Some of the other yachts had been badly damaged. Christie was glad to see Philip. She could use some help on her boat. Philip explained the situation to her. They then chalked out a plan.

Kalpana and Dilip reached Suresh's camp by early afternoon. There was trouble brewing. Suresh was worried. A large group of Tulsi tribals armed with bows and arrows had surrounded the camp. Suresh's scouts had spotted a number of other armed men in the group. These men carried automatic weapons. There had been no armed clashes between the tribes for the past 30 years. Prior to that, the history of bloodshed between the two groups stretched back to a hundred years. A Tuttu scout came running up. The Tulsi's had barricaded the camp gate from the outside. They were trapped and with no communication to the outside world.

At eleven pm Raghu and Santhamma heard the gate creak open. They remained in the living room as they had been instructed. A white ambassador car drew up at the porch with its lights doused. A man got out of it and strode into the living room, kicking the door open. It was Sumant. He raised his hand as Raghu opened his mouth to speak. Sumant carried a pistol in his gloved hand. He snapped open his briefcase and tossed two sets of documents to Raghu and Santhamma. "Sign it", he ordered.

Christie's rescheduled race was about to start. The unseasonal storm had abated. There was a blue sky overhead with not a trace of a cloud. She had taken on Philip, Hemant and Supriya as crew. Philip was an accomplished sailor. Hemant had sailed boats at the defense academy. Supriya was an absolute novice and did not even know how to swim. She insisted on going along. She would have to keep out of the other's way, keep her head down and learn as they sailed along. They had worn the sailing colors of Christie's team. With yachting caps pulled over their heads they were not easy to recognize. The race area was a hundred nautical miles from where the Celestra was located. They planned to stray off course and head for the Celestra pretending to have rudder damage from the earlier storm.

The sea was still a trifle choppy as the starter's flag went down. The flotilla of boats with their multicoloured sails sailed out on the first leg of the race. Sumitra was tossed about in the boat, but the spray in her face and the wind in her hair kept her from being sea sick. Christie was at the helm. Philip and Hemant worked the sails. They raced the first leg in earnest and were in the leading lot of boats when they abruptly suddenly tacked away on a new course. A jury boat pulled up alongside. Christie pleaded rudder damage. They would forfeit the race. They declined the offer for assistance. They would repair the damage themselves. The jury boat left. They headed straight to where the Celestra1 and her fishing boats were operating. When they were about ten nautical miles away from the area, they hoisted a distress flag. Soon they could see the fishing fleet.

Suresh, Kalpana and Dilip were huddled with the tribals of the camp. They were hopelessly outnumbered. They guessed that the attack would come late at night. That was how the Tulsi tribe operated. They would start drinking toddy and Ganja from the late evening and then attack in a state of utter inebriation. This made them ferocious and merciless. They would murder and rape without compunction. One of Tuttu trackers, Ramba had a plan. He knew of a cave in the hill behind the camp. If they could get to the cave through a secret jungle path that he knew of, there was a chance that they could hide there. No one usually ventured near the cave. Kaala the python lived in it. Ramba and his family had been giving the python milk and chickens every morning. Maybe the snake would spare them. They all agreed that Kaala was more likely to show them mercy than the Tulsi.

As Raghu read the papers his son gave him to sign, his blood froze. It was a detailed confession, giving dates and figures on how Raghu and Santhamma had masterminded the terror strikes. It was very believable and forgeries were convincing. He looked at his son. Sumant's gun was pointed unwaveringly at Santhamma's head. He signed the confession. Santhamma had already signed her forms. They watched in silence as Sumant opened his brief case and kept the papers in them. Sumant took a step to the door and opened it. He looked around outside and then turned back lifting his gun and pointing it at Raghu's head. Santhamma screamed. The silenced gun coughed once. Ragu's lifeless body slid to the ground. There was a neat bullet hole between his eyes. Sumant turned the gun on Santhamma. She had slid to the ground and was whimpering in the corner. There was a blur of black fur as Stephan, Philip's dog jumped at Sumant from the open door. He had broken his leash. His teeth clamped into Sumant's forearm, crushing bone and severing his radial artery. The gun clattered to the ground. Howling in fear and anguish Sumant jumped upon the table. His brief case fell to the ground, the impact jarring it open, sending the papers fluttering all over the room.

Santhamma had fainted. Her scream had alerted the neighbours. When a group of them gathered the courage to come and investigate, they found Raghu's lifeless body on the ground. Sathamma was sitting by his side crying. Sumant was still on the table, clutching his bleeding arm. Whenever he moved, Stephen snarled. Someone alerted the police. Sumant was arrested and then taken to hospital. His hand had turned blue and would need to be amputated. Santhamma was taken to hospital where she required sedation. Her statement and that of the neighbours was damning evidence against Sumant. He would spend the rest of his life in jail after he got out of hospital.

When Christie's boat neared the fishing fleet, a fastfishing boat came up. There was a man brandishing an automatic weapon standing on the deck. There were nets in the area, he yelled. He asked them to steer clear. Christie made a helpless gesture. Her rudder was broken. The boat was not in control. They needed assistance. There was a pause as the men on board radioed the Celeste for instructions. The yachts sail number was being noted. Philips guessed that the Celeste would be verifying if they were genuinely a part of the starting line up of the race. They seemed to have received some confirmation. Christie was instructed to lower her sail and accept the tow rope.

Under tow, they headed towards the Celeste. They wondered what was in store. Knowing the Celeste's antecedents, they guessed that they would be interrogated and killed. Their boat would be sunk. It would be made to look like a sailing accident. Hemant and Supriya had smeared sunscreen on their faces and had pulled their yachting caps low over their eyes. The fishing boat crew did not know them. But there might be someone on the Celeste who might recognize them.

Under cover of darkness, Ramba lead Suresh and the others in camp through a secret path in the forest. They had left the cooking fires burning in the huts to convey the impression that the camp was still occupied. At the base of the hill Ramba pushed aside the bushes to reveal the entrance of the rock cave. They walked into the cave. Suresh was in the lead and he put on his flash light. With the shrubbery covering the caves mouth, the light would not be seen by the Tulsi.

 The cave mouth was narrow. Inside however it was more capacious. Two men could walk abreast comfortably. The cave seemed to lead on right into the hill. Ahead, they could hear the sound of running water. This was a good sign. If there was a stream in the cave, there had to be another exit. The cave dipped and turned sharply to the right. Suddenly there was a loud hiss and a heavy body slid off a ledge. Ahead, in the light of Suresh's torch was the largest and angriest snake that they had ever seen. He had raised his head and glared at them. Nudging Suresh aside, Ramba stepped forward. He took the torch from Suresh's hand and turned it upon himself and then on the rest of the group. The snake seemed to relax. He lowered his head and got back on his ledge. Ramba gestured to the rest of the group to follow him. They walked in a single file past the majestic creature.

There was a loud whoop from the cave mouth. The Tulsi had detected their escape and had found the cave. Kaala raised his head in anger. The distant glow of torches could be seen. As the screeching Tulsis rushed in, Kaala waited, his mouth wide open. The first Tulsi turned the corner, his raised machete thirsting for blood. Kaala struck. The Tulsi following him saw a frightening sight. Kaala was swallowing the man whole. His head and shoulders were in the snake's mouth, while his feet thrashed around in agony. There were screams. The Tulsi dropped their torches and ran, stumbling over one another in fright. Suresh and his group had reached the flowing water of the stream. They were soon wading through knee deep water. Ahead of them was the sound of a waterfall. The current was stronger.

 Fortunately, there was a rocky path by the stream's side. In a single line and holding each other's hand the chain of escapees reached the caves mouth. The moon had come out by now and the sheer beauty of the cascading water was breathtaking. There was no path down. There was a sloping rock to their left and beyond that there was some vegetation. Suresh and his group climbed the rock. Ahead of them, beyond a grassy slope was the highway. There was a whoop of joy from the group. They had escaped.

Christie and her crew were at the Celeste. A hatch had opened and two armed men escorted them up the ladder and to the captain's cabin. They would soon learn the identity of the octopus. The guards halted on either side of the cabin door. They gestured for Christie and her group to enter. Christie had already moved into the room when Hemant had a glimpse at the occupant of the captain's chair. It was Sitara. She was dressed in a suit. On either side of her was an armed woman. The women were tall and stately. They wore jump suits and carried automatic pistols. Hemant motioned to Supriya to stay back and whispered in Philip' ear as he was entering. "It is Sitara". Philip pulled the cap low over his eyes and entered. Hemant pretended to stumble and bent down to tie his shoe lace.

 Sitara motioned for Christie and Philip to sit down. Christie sat. Philip seemed to loose his footing as he pulled his chair. One of the armed women moved forward to steady him. In a trice Philip wrenched the pistol from her holster. Vaulting over the table, he held the pistol to Sitara's head. As the other armed woman tried to draw her pistol, Christie jumped her. They fell together to the floor. Christie was a karate black belt. She rose, holding the pistol, while her opponent remained immobile on the floor.

Hearing the commotion, the two guards moved into the cabin. Hemant rose from his slouch. His elbow behind the second guard's ear knocked the man unconscious. Hemant grabbed the man's rifle and with a vicious swipe of its butt felled the first guard. Then there was a sudden silence. Supriya had entered the room now. Sitara's face was a mask of hatred and frustration. She was standing now with Philip's powerful arm round her neck and his pistol on her temple. There was a door behind Sitara's chair and from behind that door they heard a child's cry.

Supriya ran to the door and wrenched it open. There was Sheshank. His arms were strapped to the chair. He smiled when he saw his mother. The boy had nerves of steel. They untied him and then he was in his mother's arms, both of them crying tears of joy. The group moved to the ships bridge. Philip still had his pistol at Sitara's head. He turned the Celeste eastward and gunned her engines. The fishing fleet followed in hot pursuit.

When Santhamma recovered her composure, she phoned up Maninder. She told him the whole story. Suresh, Dilip and Kalpana were also safe. Sankaran Kutty was arrested as he tried to flee the country at the Goa airport. Then there was a message for Dilip from Philip. They heard him whoop with joy as he got the news. The Celeste was under their control. Sheshank was safe. Maninder got the defence minister to order a naval frigate, to escort the Celeste into Bombay harbour. The other fishing boats which had been chasing them scattered when they saw the naval frigate.

Maninder was there at Raghu's final rites with the rest of them. After the ashes had been scattered, they drove back to the Government house. There was a statue to be unveiled in front of the old Teak building. Maninder had got it sculpted on hearing of Raghu's demise. The inscription on the statue read, 'Raghunath of Rajbhavan".

The Seller of Blessings

Chapter 1   Swami Achutan

Swami Achuthan was the chief priest at the Godavakari temple. His father and grandfather both had been in charge of the temple before him. The deity of the Godavakari temple was ideosyncratic. He relaxed for most of the year. But come September and his powers flourished. At this time devotees thronged the temple. There was no wish that was denied, miracles were the norm. News of this great power spread all through the land. The queues were long with sick people who came for healing, infertile couples who came for a child and the poor who came for wealth. The blind saw, the lame walked and the lines became longer. The devotees returned with generous gifts and offerings.

There was a temple trust which handled the finances of the temple. The trust was rich and they invested wisely. There was money kept aside for temple maintenance. Hotels were put up by the trust for the devotees and these hotels earned the trust even more money. Money, like infamy nurtures itself.

Swami Achuthan also prospered. The gold offerings were for the Gods. The priest however decided the place an offering would have in the sanctum sanctorum. Devotees soon knew that if their gift had to find the eyes of the deity, Achuthan had to be appeased with a generous 'Kaineetam' or gift. Over a period of time Achuthan became very wealthy.

Being a man of God, Achuthan feared no one except the revenue department officials. It was a ridiculous state of affairs, thought Achuthan, when he had to pay taxes for gifts received in the temple. Nothing was sacred anymore. It was tantamount to taxing God. The law of the land, thought Achuthan was above the realm of God. He considered the revenue department to be a plague of leeches.

Achutan knew of another Swami from a nearby temple who had not offered a place of prominence to a man's gold offering. What else did the man expect after giving a kaineetam of five rupees? The man had turned out to be a revenue officer. He had put an operative to observe the number and value of tips the swami received every day. He had then stuck a tax recovery order with penalties for tax evasion on the priest. For months on end he had to pay obeisance to the official, giving generous gifts to all in the department before a more realistic evaluation was made. It was more difficult to appease a revenue official than to appease Shiva.

Achuthan had only one son. His name was Purushothaman. Purushothaman or Paru as he was often called was in many ways a disappointment. Paru went to the local government school. In the mornings he would assist Achuthan in temple work before running off for his classes. There was no reason for him to take classes as seriously as he did. The errant lad stayed up late into the night burning midnight oil learning science and the arts. He seemed oblivious of the fact that he had a lucrative priesthood waiting for him. "Paru should realize that he was born a prince", thought Achuthan.

With a basic education he could have moved in as Achuthan's assistant and one day taken his place at the sanctum. Achuthan was making more money and earned more respect than any doctor or engineer in the state. 'It was his mother's influence", thought Achuthan. She was the one was so happy when Paru topped his class or won an award for the best science project.

Chapter 2   Purushothaman

Paru was adamant about continuing his education and his mother was supporting him. He finished his school setting new records in the science subjects. There were students from other schools who had better marks than him. Paru however was sure than none of these children had had to assist in the puja and wash the temple steps even on the day of their examinations. Paru was devout enough. It was just that he had a thirst for knowledge and learning that seemed insatiable. His school syllabus had given him a glimpse of the ocean of knowledge. He pursued his studies with passion.

Achuthan was finally convinced that Paru would never take his place in the temple. He needed an heir. There was a nephew whose studies he had sponsored out of his generosity. The boy however had refused to attend school after class five and was now sitting idle at home. Achuthan took over his temple training. The chief priesthood should not be lost to the family.

Paru joined the regional engineering college at Trichur. He had chosen telecommunications as his subject. The initial few days at the college hostel were hell for him. Ragging of the fresher batch was unbridled and crude. His seniors had made him strip and subjected him to all sorts of humiliation. He was finally saved by Kanchi Ram. Kanchi Ram was final year engineering student. He was also the president of the student council. Kanchiram was a Brahmin and was also known to have the support of the local RSS, a militant Hindu organization. He heard of this young Brahmin boy who was being tortured and decided to take him under his wing. The goons now backed off. If they tangled with Kanchi, it would be unsafe for them outside the college gates.

Paru now had more time to devote to his studies than his fellow students who were still being ragged. He spent his free time in the library. His assignments were always complete on time. His professors adored him. In most professional courses, an academic hierarchy is created within a few months of commencement. This hierarchy is often retained till the completion of the course. Paru's strong start stood him in good stead. He sailed through engineering college in a blaze of glory. Success never intoxicated him. He continued to display a disciplined austerity and rigorous ascetism which at once made him an object of admiration and of ridicule.

 Paru performed his prayers with diligence and cultivated none of the vices that were rampant on the engineering college campus. His friends had fancy motorcycles and roamed around on them with their girl-friends attached. Paru commuted on a bicycle. He never wore jeans or T shirts and despite Kanchi Ram's encouragement did not dabble in politics.

Paru graduated on top of his class. There were great opportunities coming up in the telecom sector. Mobile telephones had just entered the Indian market and the oncoming boom would be astronomical. Paru could join a telecom major straightaway or he could complete his 'Masters in Business Administration' and join in a managerial appointment. Paru surprised everyone by doing neither. There was a non-governmental organization, the 'Grameen Vikas Sangh' which was focusing on bringing technology to the villages of India. They were looking for young engineers to help them fulfil their mission. His father was unhappy at the decision. If Paru had wanted to do social service, he could have stayed on in the temple. What was the use of doing an engineering course if one were planning to work in the village anyway? His specialization in telecom could hardly be of benefit in rural India where motorable roads, electrification and water supply were undreamt of luxuries. His mother did not comment. She appreciated his idealism. She knew how committed Paru was to dreams. She could only pray that her son's ideals and dreams attained fruition.

Paru moved to Madhukarai. He was to take up his appointment in a tribal village about fifty-five kilometres from Madhukarai city. The tribal settlement of the Thekkandi could be reached only by a mud track. He was driven there by an irate representative of the Grameen Sangh. The tribals in the settlement were thieves and robbers he told Paru. If they did not want to escape their squalor, what could anyone else do? Many aid agencies had come and gone. They had made no difference to the tribal's lives.

Paru met Ponkula, the tribal chieftain. Ponkula did not appear overtly enthused with Grameen Sangh's new initiative. There had been similar initiatives earlier. He had seen too many failed aid schemes. There would be an inauguration with a lot of fanfare and the inevitable hordes of photo and videographers. There would be handouts of old clothes and nutritional food supplements for children. All this would last a week or two. Then the aid agency would lose interest and the settlement would be the same again.

There was no potable water in the village. There was a pipeline which delivered water to the nearby township of Ramaji. Water was aplenty there. The Ramaji folk were however upper-class Hindus and they refused to share the same water supply with some 'untouchable' tribals. For the same reason, buses that plied from Madhukarai to Ramaji could not pick up passengers from the tribal settlement. Tribals from the settlement were not allowed to pass through the Ramaji village. They had to walk down a mud track to the highway which was a good ten kilometers away, where a contractor's truck would pick them up to ferry them to Madhukarai. Here, the men worked as construction labourers.

The Grameen Sangh had been founded by a politician. After the initial hype and publicity, he withdrew his active patronage. The batch of talented youngsters he had recruited would have to do it on their own. Fortunately, the World Bank had agreed to fund the venture for the next three years. The engineers would not starve. They would get a monthly remuneration and they could apply for funds for infrastructure development projects in the villages. The newspapers had initially covered the organizations activities, but with political participation waning they shifted their focus to other fields. Some of the engineers resigned. They realized that they had made an initial bad career decision and would restart their careers. A few, stayed on. There were no new joiners except for Paru.

The agent who took him around suggested that Paru stay in the Ramaji town. He suggested that Paru stay there. It was closer than Madhukarai. He would have the Sangh's jeep to drive to the settlement when required. After the meeting with Ponkulam, the agent had briefed him on the problems they faced in the settlement. A previous worker had tried to get a school building built for the tribals. Land was available. Truckloads of cement and bricks had been dumped at the site for construction. But before the work could start, the bricks had disappeared. The tribals were thieves.

The last engineer had given up the project and had soon resigned. It was not safe to venture into the village alone. There was always an undercurrent of caste animosity. Maybe Paru should not display the holy thread he wore around his neck so proudly. That could make him a target for the tribals. The agent had checked Paru into a hotel at Ramaji. The official jeep was given for servicing and would be ready the next morning.

When he went down for dinner, the hotel proprietor made polite conversation. He was surprised to hear that Paru was the son of Achuthan the high priest. Surely the Brahmin would not want to desecrate himself by working for the scheduled castes in the settlement. With all the government's populist reservation policies, there would be enough low caste engineers for these jobs. Maybe Paru had not got another job, he suggested. He was welcome to stay at the hotel, provided he kept his contact with the settlement at a minimum.

There was a village well at outskirts of Ramaji that the scheduled castes were not allowed to use. He could wash his feet there before re-entering the town. Paru listened in silence. The next morning, he went down to the garage to collect the jeep. News of the Brahmin who had come to help the Thekkandi's had spread. They all looked upon Paru as some kind of a freak. "The World Bank was a good milking cow", said the Garage foreman. If Paru played his cards well, he could have a good life and maybe even divert some development funds to Ramaji.

Chapter 3   Paru moves to Thekkandi.

Paru now drove his jeep down to the Thekkandi settlement. There was hardly a road to speak of and the ten kilometers took him almost an hour. There was no motorable road to the inside of the settlement. An empty canal separated a coconut grove from the first row of huts. He parked his jeep in the coconut grove. A young lady walked past him carrying a pot of water on her hip and another balanced on her head. "Where does Ponkulam Live?" he called out to her. She ignored him completely and walked on into the village.

Paru followed her. There were two village lads playing cards in the shade of a grass thatch. "Where does Ponkulam stay?" he repeated the question to them. The youths pointed after the lady with the water pots. "She is Ponkulam's daughter. Follow her", said one youth. The other youth did not even look up. The girl had not shown any sign of having heard them. Wordlessly Paru hurried after her. At the door of a grass thatched house in the centre of the village she paused. For the first time she looked at Paru.

She was beautiful and dark with sharp features, unusual for a lady from the tribes. Her eyes flashed the suggestion of a smile and there was a hint of pearly white teeth. She pointed to a charpoy near the hut's entrance. "Please sit on it" she said in perfect English, "I will call my father".

Ponkulam came out of his house wearing multi coloured shorts. He was not wearing a shirt today. There were many scars of old feuds tattooed on his chest and back. Ponkulam was surprised to see him. When he heard Paru's proposition, he was incredulous. "A Brahmin staying in the Tuttu colony?" he burst out laughing. "Swapna", he called out to his daughter. The girl peeped out. "This Brahmin wants to stay in the Thekkandi colony and work for us". He was mocking Paru. Swapna sprang to Paru's defense. "There are good people in the world", she told her father. "Why don't you let him do what he wants to? Shakur's hut which is next to ours is lying vacant".

Swapna was addressing Paru now. "Come tomorrow and the hut will be ready for you" she said. Ponkula nodded his assent. "How have you come?" he asked Paru. Swapna answered for him, "By jeep. I will bet my kitchen stove that everything including the wheels would have been stolen off it by now."

Ponkula accompanied Paru to the coconut grove. Swapna was right. The jeep had been ransacked. One of the youths he had seen earlier was wheeling the last tire off when they reached. Ponkula was furious. "I will be having a cup of tea with my friend in my house", he yelled. "When I come back with him if the Jeep is not fully restored I will pluck your eyes out and feed them to the crows". They walked back to Paru's hut. Swapna had already prepared tea for them in mud cups.

Ponkula advised Paru to reconsider his plans. If he stayed in the Thekkandi colony, the upper caste Hindus would never forgive him. His life could be in danger. Paru had however made up his mind and he would not budge from his plan. When they went back to the grove, the jeep parts had all been replaced. "He is my new son". Ponkula told the surprised youths. "He will be staying in Shakur's hut. Make a track for him to drive his jeep till there".

The next morning Paru moved into the Thekkandi colony, ignoring the threats and jibes of the Ramaji townsmen. "If you set foot in this town again you will not live to regret it", they warned him. Paru realized that they were serious.

When Paru reached the settlement with his luggage, he was guided to his new hut. He found it clean and ready for inhabitation. There was a crude charpoy and a mat in the corner. A small kerosene stove, a couple of cooking vessels, a glass and a plate waited for him on a wooden ledge. Near the charpoy, there was a also a mud pot with drinking water. There was a knock on the door. A smiling Ponkula stood there with Swapna. "She did up the hut for you", said Ponkula with a smile. Swapna took him around and showed him the village well where he could have a bath. She would get him drinking water from a well outside the settlement. This water was sweeter, "Sweeter than water in the Ramaji town", said Ponkula with a smirk. There was a row of broken-down toilets near the edge of the settlement. But most of the villagers used the fields around.

Paru spent the next few days learning the ways of the village. The men would leave early in the morning for Madhukarai where they worked as construction workers or casual labourers. It was a long walk across the fields to the highway where the contractor's trucks would wait for them. In the evening, they returned the same way. The women stayed at home doing cooking and cleaning. They ventured out to fetch water from the village well in the outskirts and for tending to their children's needs.

Till a few years ago, the women used to go to work too. They were hardy women and they would work hard. However, they were naïve and easily exploited. After a couple of nasty incidents Ponkula had passed the order that women would not go for work outside the settlement. There was no school for the children. An open-air school had been started by a Christian group a year ago. The government had shut it down under pressure from the Hindu groups. Ther were fears that the school might become a platform for conversions.

Chapter 4   Paru starts his Work

 In the evening Paru sat on the charpoy outside Ponkula's hut and together they discussed Paru's plans for the settlement. Paru wanted to restart the school. He could help out with the science subjects, but if he spent all his time at school the other projects would not take off. He could buy the books and slates, but who would do the teaching? Ponkula looked at Swapna. Swapna spoke up. She had been in the city of Chennai with her mother till a couple of years ago. Her mother had worked in one of the schools there as a sweeper. Swapna had studied in the school and completed her twelfth. Two years ago her mother had died in a tragic accident. Swapna had then returned to the settlement to stay with her father. She would take over the school if her father agreed. Ponkula thought for a minute and then agreed. Swapna would have to group the children according to their age and prior schooling. She would have to move from one one group to the other till a new set of teachers were ready. Till the she would manage, teaching and giving assignments.

The next morning Paru took his jeep and drove to Madhukarai town. He took the same route as the other villagers. He went to the local school book stall and bought what he thought was a reasonable supply of school books, slate and chalks. He also bought some sweets for the children as inducements to come to school. He shot off a letter to the world bank describing the conditions of the village. He also gave a broad sketch of what could be done to effect development. He then drove back to the village and reached by mid afternoon.

Swapna had prepared lunch for him. There was a letter from his father. He read it after returning to his hut. His father had come to know that he was living in the Thekkandi village. Henceforth he would not consider Paru his son. He had found an heir in Gopal who would one day take over as the chief priest. Paru had expected this. He wondered how his mother was taking it. He would phone her up when his father was not around and speak to her.

The school was a great hit. The children came for the chocolates, but stayed on for the learning. There was soon a shortage of slates and chalks. Many of the older children had to write their lessons in the mud. He would have to pick up some more slates and chalk from Madhukarai. A letter came in from the World Bank official. The regional director, a man named Philips would come down to

Madhukarai village the coming Wednesday. Paru was to go and meet him at the resort hotel at two in the afternoon.

The Ramaji's had come to know of Paru's letter and of the appointment he had with the World Bank man. A Ramaji man was a clerk in the World Bank office. He supplied all the details to the town's elders. They decided that they could not afford to let the plans go ahead. They chalked out their moves. Paru meanwhile prepared his presentation. A small book was prepared giving the history of the Thekkandis. He described the caste system and the indignities the tribals suffered daily. He described the pathetic lining conditions in the settlement.

The Thekkandi had been forest dwellers earlier, but with the forest lands being taken over by an industrial concern, they had been relocated to the settlement. Paru wanted photographs of the settlement, but there was no place where he could charge his camera. He and Swapna got the school children to make drawings of various aspects of village life. Finally, the proposals were complete and the drawings incorporated. "It is a work of art", said Paru proudly. The World Bank would be impressed.

Chapter 5   The Ambush

Wednesday morning, armed with this work of art, he set out for Madhukarai. The village men had already left. He drove his jeep down the mud track. There was a sharp turn in the road as it turned around a hillock. Turning the corner, he had to brake suddenly. There was a tree that had fallen across the road. A van was parked on the other side. Six people armed with lathis stepped out of the van. Paru was trapped.

The Ramaji goons jumped upon him and dragged him out of the jeep. They thrashed him soundly. The goons then threw him into an empty well. They set his jeep on fire. It was to look like an accident. The police would state that the jeep had veered off the road and fallen into the well, where it burst into flames. They tried to push in the burning jeep after Paru into the well. The jeep was in gear and they had to use a lathi to shift the gear to neutral. Their timing went a awry. The jeep had to be pushed around the fallen tree trunk. Before it reached the well's edge it exploded. Two of the Ramaji goons were badly burnt. The goons panicked.

Leaving Paru in the well, they jot into the van and fled with their injured friends. They planned to come back later to finish off the renegade Brahmin. They would need kerosene and torches.

Paru had lost consciousness when he fell into the well. A bush growing from the well's wall had broken his fall. Slowly he came to his senses. He could vaguely hear someone calling his name from the well's mouth.

It was Swapna. She had been in the village watching the puff of dust as Paru's jeep headed for Madhukarai. Then the dust cloud had stopped. Swapna had walked to the settlement's edge wondering if Paru's jeep had broken down. Then there was an explosion. She ran towards the hillock. By the time she reached the spot, his assailants had fled.

Swapna had heard groans coming from the well and then seen him. She called out to him. Paru was sitting up now. There was a rope that the Ramaji's had used to pull the Jeep towards the well. Tying one end of the rope to a tree she threw the other end down to Paru. The rope was too short. She pulled the rope back up. Swapna looked around. There was no one in sight. She took off her Sari and tied it to the ropes end. She then lowered the rope again. Paru could reach the lifeline now. Slowly, he climbed out of the well.

 The sun was almost overhead. He remembered his appointment with the World Bank official. If they missed the appointment, they would probably never get such a chance again. They must somehow reach Madhukarai before the World Bank official left. Paru and Sapna ran for the road. They flagged down a passing truck.

The driver refused to take them as they had no money with them. They pleaded with him. He agreed after Swapna took off her gold ring and gave it to him. The truck dropped the duo at the outskirts of Madhukarai. It was already four o'clock. They ran towards the hotel.

They could see the fifteen storied structure in the distance. As they turned into the road in front of the hotel, they were in for a shock. A group of Ramaji goons armed with lathis stood at the hotels gate. The men had also seen them. Ther was a shout and the goons started running down the road towards the couple. The hotels lawns lay to their left. There was a high wall that would be impossible to climb over. They were in luck. There was a locked service gate of the hotel to their left. Paru and Swapna jumped over the gate and started running across the lawns.

Ahead of them at the hotel porch, they could see a luxury van with the World Bank insignia on it. A well built Englishman was getting into the car. Philips, the World Bank man had given up waiting. Behind them, the Ramaji goons had already climbed over the gate and were hot on their heels. The van was leaving the porch now. Paru and Swapna ran towards the car waving their arms wildly. Philips saw the running couple and the goons with lathis after them. He told the driver to stop the van and opened the door. The couple jumped in. The van shot off again.

Inside the van, Paru introduced himself and Swapna to the banker. He told him of the proposal they had prepared, about the attack and the burnt jeep. Philip had a solution. He directed the driver to follow Paru's instructions and drive to the settlement. They were back on the mud track. They saw the skeleton of Paru's jeep by the track. The burnt jeep was still smoking. Thankfully some returning Thekkandi men had removed the fallen tree to the roadside.

They reached the settlement without trouble. Paru introduced Ponkula to Philips. They took Philip for a tour around the settlement. He showed Philip the open-air school. Paru then explained his proposals to Philips. He explained his plan for pumping water from the wells to overhead tanks and the creation of a water distribution system. There could be a system of windmills for the generation of electricity, which could serve as a model for the rest of the country. He proposed a whole new township design. It was an ambitious plan. Paru however had managed to convince Philip. He left with a quiver of proposals under his arm. He would try to get the projects accepted as soon as possible.

Chapter 6   The Ramaji's Attack

That night the Ramajis attacked. A Thekkandi youth came running to Ponkula's house with the news. A convoy of trucks was headed towards them from the Ramaji town. Paru and Ponkula ran to the edge of the clearing. The trucks were about five kilometers away by now. Ponkula was a seasoned warrior of many campaigns and he chalked out a war plan.

 The Ramajis would have to park their trucks in the coconut grove. A dozen men hid in the thicket around the grove. Meanwhile Swapna led the women and children away to hide in the sugarcane fields behind the village. The shrubbery was dense here and as the fields belonged to the Ramajis they would not raze them down in a hurry. A group of Tuttus with bows and arrows climbed up a hillock by the settlement. Another large group lay concealed in the empty irrigation ditch by the settlements edge.

Ther were about two hundred Ramaji in the ten trucks. The Tuttu village seemed eerily silent. They guessed that the residents were sleeping. Jumping off their trucks, with their flaming torches and firing their guns they charged at the settlement. The men were drunk and excited at the prospect of loot and rape.

As they cleared the embankment a shower of arrows from the hill caught them by surprise. There were screams of agony from the injured. The men turned, sensing a challenge from the hills. They fired their guns into the hills, but the Thekkandi were well concealed. "Douse the torches", someone screamed. "The lights make us easy targets for the arrows". The torches were doused and the men charged uphill. The concealed contingent of Thekkandi warriors let them pass and then were upon them, with their spears and short knifes. At this range, guns were useless and the tribals knew the terrain. It was a blood bath. There was a flash of fire as one of the trucks caught fire and then the other. The Thekkandi hiding in the coconut grove had done their work. The Ramajis panicked and ran, dragging their dead and wounded.

There were no more attacks at night, but the women and children spend the night in the fields. The news of the carnage spread. A battalion of police surrounded the camp in the morning. They rounded up all the able-bodied men and herded them off to jail. They then cordoned off the village. Both Paru and Ponkula were amongst those taken. Swapna knew what the police planned to do. They would lift the cordon at night and go to Ramaji. There they would change into local attire and return to the settlement with the Ramaji to help them in their revenge.

She planned their escape. All families had kept their provisions ready and packed. The moment the police posse pulled out, they headed through the sugarcane fields and into the forest. It was a three-hour walk, but fear gave them wings. Once they reached the forest, they would be safe. The Thekkandi were children of the forests and no sane men would dare pursue them there. There were still scattered groups of Thekkandi who continued to live in the forest despite the government's attempts at evicting them. The leader of the group was Ponkula's brother.

They had left the kitchen fires on in the settlement to convey the impression that that the huts were still inhabited. When the attackers came at night, they found no one in the settlement. They set fire to the huts and left.

Paru had managed to send off a detailed missive to Philip after the first attack, before he was taken into police custody. Philips sent off a detailed report of the incident with a scathing indictment of the caste system to the world press and to the Indian government. He had all the colony photographs to prove that the settlement was not a Tamil separatist training camp as the local officials had tried to insinuate. The government was embarrassed. The Thekkandi were released from police captivity.

Tents were constructed for them by the army to house them till their burnt huts were rebuilt. Food delivery was arranged from Madhukarai. A contingent of the army was stationed between the two groups and asked to set up base there. The army would not bow to communal pressures and their presence was an absolute guarantee of peace.

Philips came again to their settlement a week later. He had good news. The World Bank had agreed to finance the project as a model venture. Paru would have to oversee the reconstruction. The final blueprint would need to be readied in a week.

Chapter 7   The Rebuilding

Paru detailed the planned construction of a mini township. Rows of small houses were to be located around a central common area where the school, a tribal handicraft centre and a few shops would be located. Piped water from two tube wells would provide potable water supply. A row of windmills was planned around the village would provide for eco-friendly power generation. A friend of his from the engineering college was now working with a Dutch firm which specialized in this technology and Paru had already got in touch with him. A wireless station would be established for connectivity.

A road connecting the settlement to Madhukarai city was to be made and a self-financing bus service would be started. The plan was ambitious and audacious. The sympathy wave on the burning of the settlement by the Ramaji's and the international outcry against the caste system helped sway world opinion. The project was sanctioned. Philip had ensured that the construction was contracted to an Indian firm of international standing. The firm was happy with the positive publicity they would get through the implementation of this World Bank scheme. Paru got the firm to employ Thekkandy workers in the reconstruction scheme. He would ensure that they did quality work. He also got the firm to arrange evening vocational classes for the workers and handicraft classes for the women as part of the deal. By the time the project work was completed, the Thekkandi folk would have employable skills.

Under Paru's supervision the work progressed and targets were met ahead of schedule. The project was completed in eighteen months. It was a compact yet magnificent township. The school and the handicrafts centre shifted to their new locations. The town bus with its trained Thekkandi driver was in place. The houses were handed over to the new owners in a simple but well publicized ceremony

The World Bank president had flown down for the occasion. A golden key was handed over to Ponkula. The township of Ponnadu or golden country was born. The press and the dignitaries left by evening. Paru retired to his house. He was content. He tried to, but could not get to sleep. The events of the last two years kept unfolding before his eyes. He thought of Swapna. Her sheer dynamism had ensured the success of the school and the handicrafts centre. It was past midnight. The lights in the houses around had been put off.

Chapter 8   Paru gets a Visitor

Paru was tossing about in his bed. He wished that the medical store was open. He desperately needed a sleeping pill. There was a soft knock on his door. It was Swapna. As he opened the door she moved into his arms. "I have waited for you for two years", she said. "If I don't become yours today, I will die, she said".

 They woke up early the next morning. Swapna dressed and went to her house. Ponkula was already up. He would have guessed where Swapna had spent the night. Paru too got ready and went to Ponkula's house. When Ponkula opened the door, he touched his feet. "I wish to marry your daughter", he said. Ponkula held him in a tight hug, warm tears of affection flowing down his weather-beaten face.

Paru and Swapna did not want an elaborate ceremony. There had been enough activity in the settlement recently. They would register their marriage in a simple Thekkandi ceremony. They were married the next day. Ponkula gifted the couple a small car as his wedding present.

 Paru had had no communication with his father for almost two years. He would phone up his mother at home whenever he got a chance. If his father came to know that his mother still spoke to him it would be bad for her. He wanted his mother's blessings for his marriage. He rang up their house. Fortunately his mother picked up the phone. Paru told her all that had transpired. She had heard about the township's creation from newspaper reports. She was proud of her son. She was worried at to how Achutan would respond.

When Achutan reached home that evening, his wife told him of their son's marriage. Achuthan hurled abuses at her and left the house. He contacted Gopal. There was a militant Brahmin organization which would help them to get their revenge. They made their plan to avenge the community's honour.

Achutan went back to his house only three days later. His fearful wife opened the door, half expecting to be beaten. But her husband seemed to be a changed man. He had brought home a packet of milk sweets in celebration of his son's wedding. "I was meditating at the sanctum for the past two days", he told his wife. "Today I got my answer. Paru is still my son and I will make his wife my daughter". His wife fell sobbing at his feet. Only God could have influenced her husband. Achuthan was still talking. "Tomorrow we will go to bless the young couple", he said. The family would get together at a five-star hotel in Madhukarai. It would be inappropriate for them to go to the Thekkandi town.

Ecstatically she called up Paru. She told him of Achuthan's meditation and his change of mind. She spoke to Swapna, calling her 'daughter' again and again till they both laughed in joy. She finalized the plans. The couple would drive down to Madhukarai in Paru's new car. Achuthan and she would wait for them at the hotel's foyer. They would have breakfast together and spend the rest of the day talking. When Paru told Ponkula of the turn of events, he was initially suspicious. But Paru was adamant. He loved and trusted his mother. She would never be party to a plot to harm him.

Chapter 9   The Betrayal

Early the next morning Swapna and Paru got ready to drive to Madhukarai. Paru wore a traditional mundu and a silk shirt. Swapna looked strikingly beautiful in a bright red silk sari. Paru's mother had rung up early in the morning. They were setting out to Madhukarai and would be there in about three hours.

After she had made the phone call Paru's mother got ready to leave. Achuthan remembered the box of sweets that they had not opened. He took out one sweet and fed it to his wife. He had made a vow that he would not eat till he saw his son. The car had come to take them to Madhukarai, but there was a little delay. Achuthan had forgotton to hand over the treasury key to Gopal. He would be back in five minutes. He left in the car. After he left the house, Paru's mother got up and latched the door. She was feeling sleepy. Maybe she could rest a while till Achuthan came back.

She lay down on the sofa and drifted off to sleep. She woke up in anguish two hours later. Her breathing was becoming difficult and there was a feeling of constriction in her chest. Achuthan was nowhere around and the front door was closed. Realization struck her. She had been poisoned. Her son would be in danger. She had to warn him. She tried to drag herself to the phone. A spasm of vomiting threw her to the floor. Her head temporarily cleared. The telephone was only four feet away, and she managed to reach it with a superhuman effort. She rang up Paru's number, but could not get through.

 She remembered Swapna's number and tried to ring her up. Ponkula picked up the phone. Swapna had not taken her cell phone with her. Her voice was weak and the words came in short gasps. Ponkula realized that it was Paru's mother. He could barely make out what she was saying except, "they will kill him". There was a crash at the other end as she fell to the floor. She was beyond help and would die in minutes. Ponkula picked up his sword and ran to the town bus.

When Paru and Swapna reached the hotel's porch, Achuthan was there, standing next to a blue van with dark windows. Paru ran up to him and touched his feet. He looked up at his father. He was not giving him the traditional blessing. He saw the steely look in his father's eyes. In a flash, he realized that they had been trapped. Four burly men got out of the van. Paru screamed to Swapna, "Run". It was too late. The men caught them and bundled them into the van. Achuthan had walked off to another car. Paru saw that the car was driven by Gopal. The car sped away.

The van with its two prisoners on the floor boards headed in another direction. Paru's telephone rang. One of the men picked it out of his pocket. He grimaced when he saw the identity of the caller. The old coot was still alive. Quickly he made a call.

The town bus was parked at the stop. Ramdu, the driver was having tea at a nearby tea stall. "Drive to Madhukarai", Ponkula screamed, dragging the surprised man to the bus. "They will murder our children".

They set off with a screech of tires, Ramdu was pushing the engine to its limits. When they reached the hotel, the police were already there, recording evidence. The hotel security staff had alerted them to the kidnap. They had the description and the number of the van from the security men. Ponkula jumped back into the bus. By the time the cops found the van it would be too late. They had to look for it themselves. They started to search the city. They looked in parking lots and asked auto-rikshaw drivers if they had seen the blue van.

The van with its prisoners left the city premises. Soon they were on a highway. After a few minutes, they turned into a side road. A gate was opened and the van drove in. The house was empty. Paru and Swapna were dragged into the front room. Yanking off Swapna's sari, they trussed her up like a chicken and threw her into the corner. "We will first finish off the Brahmin", said the leader of the group. "Then we will have all the time for you". The others laughed.

There were iron rods and broken glass pieces lying about the front room. The men had broken in the night before and had stolen the van from the same garage. When the occupants returned from their holiday abroad, they would find the bodies. They used the rod to beat Paru to a pulp. Fortunately, the first blow was to the head and he lost consciousness. They then turned to Swapna. She was huddled in a corner and was beyond tears. One of the men lifted her on his shoulder and carried her to the bed room.

There was a crash as a heavy bus rammed through the gates. The door splintered open and Ponkula was there, with his sword. He took in the scene at a glance. A burly man was kneeling over Swapna on the bed. The others had dropped their iron rods and they were watching. Ponkula's swinging sword decapitated two of the men before they could react. The third man dived for his iron rod, but Ponkulas foot stomped down on his neck with brutal force. There was a sickening snap and the man lay still.

The man who had carried Swapna into the room had a knife in his hand. Holding the knife to her throat and keeping the girl as a shield from Ponkula he made his way to the living room.

They were at the broken glass panel door now. The man was trying to get away with Swapna as a hostage. As they passed through the broken glass door Swapna wrenched out a broken shard of glass from the frame. She plunged it with all her strength into the man's belly. There was a look of intense surprise on his face. His eyes had been fixed on Ponkula. His eyes glazed over as blood from his torn aorta flooded into his abdomen. The grip around Swapna's neck relaxed and he fell down lifeless.

They rushed to Paru. He was barely breathing. They carried him to the bus and rushed towards hospital. Swapna was giving him mouth to mouth breathing. At the hospital the doctors examined him. The pupils of his eyes were dilated and fixed. He was dead.

Chapter 10   Epilogue

Eighteen months went by. Swapna was seated in the front row of the magnificent auditorium. On one side of her was Philips. Ponkula sat on the other side, looking dapper in his suit. In her arms she carried Paru's son. He was now nine months old.

Swapna had barely spoken to anyone after Paru's murder. She had not even cried at his final rites. She refused to move in, back with her father. The school and the Handicraft's centre kept her busy. This was Paru's dream and she would keep it alive.

She was pregnant with Paru's child. Months rolled by. When he was born, she felt alive again. Some part of Paru would now always be by her side.

The master of ceremonies was announcing. "The winner of the Nobel Peace Prize for the year, awarded to Purushothaman of Grameen Vikas Sangh". There was thunderous applause. Philips escorted the widow with her infant in her arms to the podium. The gold medallion was placed around the infant's neck.

Something welled up within Swapna snapped. As she tottered Philips held her arm. Swapna had not cried since Paru's death. Now the tears started. As she sobbed Ponkula came up to the stage to support her. The hall rose in a moment of silence to honour the dead hero. The saga of Purushothaman was over.

****

Thoughts

The Entity of Excellence

The phenomenon of excellence is characterized by purity. Excellence is aspired for by the pure in spirit and achieved by purity of effort. The reward for excellence is the quest itself. I am not implying that a work looses its excellence if the reward of recognition is bestowed upon it. Neither does a pecuniary reward awarded to an artist an artist detract from the purity of the artistic creation. Excellence however cannot be achieved if the motive behind its pursuit were primarily avarice.

In a way the pursuit of excellence is a reflection of the desire for oneness with God. There is a purity of effort in the ascent towards excellence. There is also purity of motive, where the quest is reason enough. Excellence is not perfection. It is often imperfect as perfection is synonymous with confirmation with a norm. Excellence is beyond perfection. It is exciting because of its perpetual aspiration. The difference between perfection and excellence is of a true copy from an artistic original.

God is often described as perfect. He cannot be improved upon. What he was, he is and will be. God defies comprehension. Could we consider God as dynamic, constantly renewing himself, reinventing himself and manifesting in a myriad new ways. Change contradicts perfection. A dynamic God can be described as excellent and this description is ore apt than that of a static perfect entity. God is excellence and godliness, the quest of excellence. He is purer than what we can comprehend, yet perfecting his purity by the moment that is excellent. This is the purity of a dynamic perfection. Excellence is dynamic perfection.

 God is constantly reenergizing and renewing. The quest for achievement in any field is an aspiration for excellence and hence Godly. Excellence cannot be bought or inherited. It has to be achieved. If one's quest is pure, in art or sport, science or in literature, one gets nearer to God. The best method of worship is to emulate God by constantly striving to improve oneself.

Religions which profess a static doctrine of godly perfection get mired in the irrelevance of veiled irrelevance. The worship of a patriarch of dynamic excellence has to be an evolving dogma even though it may be imprudent and impudent to suggest so. Many dinosaurs have bitten the dust while cockroaches have survived and will, for ever.

Is Fairness Really Fair

The concept of fairness is nebulous. An innate understanding of fairness and justice is however universal. Fairness in battle and fairness in sport are clichéd axioms. Yet competitive sport and combat are never fair at all. Victory here is by exploitation of another's weakness. We win by our cunning and by conniving. The field of athletics is basically fair. Victory is achieved by extolling the best in self and not by exploiting the failure of another. The term fair play else where imply rule play. You play by the rules. Yet the rules permit and encourage you to cheat. We kick in a goal after distracting the goalie or bring down a boxers defense with a feint to deliver a knockout punch. Fair play is not fair at all.

Unfairness is a part of everyday life. There is little truth in the axiom of fair competition. You would not tell your rival that your girlfriend has an afternoon off. There is little merit in being squeakily fair.

At a first glance it would appear that absolute fairness is ridiculous folly. There would be too many matches lost, opportunities missed and heartaches.

Ther is however scope for absolute fairness. Athletics for example is a pure sport.. The height of unfairness here is to consume substances to assist in one's own performance enhancement. Rules are broken here. The distinction between methods of manipulating the internal milieu is tantalizingly ambiguous.

In real life, fairness is a stimulus for self enhancement. By professing the truth that another man is better to an employer or a potential mate, we take the first step toward self enhancement. Unfairness is hence illogical as it hampers accomplishment. We will measure ourselves at the end of our lives by what we are and not by how much we make. It is only fair to ourselves to explore the realm of squeaky fairness.

Interactions

It is a common phenomenon that we see in trains. Observe two people who settle down in their seats opposite one another. If they make eye contact, it often takes the form of a baleful glare. One half expects them to burst into snarls if there was the slightest provocation. Contrary to what pacifists profess, it is unwise to smile at strangers. A smile invades their privacy. It might induce them to growl. As members of a civilized society, we attempt to cover up our primitive responses with words and with rationalization. It is to wise to constantly remind ourselves that this is a façade. We are white washed cemetries of aggressive emotions. We suspend our primordial impulses by training.

If two dogs pass each other on a road, they stick to a doctrine of forced avoidance. There may be a few nasty ones who snarl at every passing canine or human. This is a trained response of a dog demonstrating that he is guarding his master. The 'honest to dog' response would be a studied avoidance unless territorial or mating issues were at stake.

When we make friends, we are indulging in pack behavior. We attempt to intimidate potential rivals by our strength in numbers or of pooled resources.

The custom of shaking hands has its origin from our unicellular ancestors who evaluated the surrounding by extending their pseudopodia. We are letting others sample our chemicals rather like a dog sniffing. We say, "Feel my chemicals, there is no adrenaline in my system, I neither want to subdue you nor am I afraid of you". The Indian 'Namaste' implies subjugation. It is more like the tail between the legs response in the canine world. If it received a similar response, it implies a mutual acceptance in abject humility. The military salute is not, as some might imply, a show of an empty hand or a peace gesture. The arm is raised to strike, draw a spear, an arrow or a sword from a shoulder scabbard. It is a challenge, "Soldier-Wanna fight?" By convention it has become the mode by which men in uniform greet each other. Presenting arms in salute, is another mode of demonstrating readiness for combat.

There is generally unanimity of opinion that goodness is what brings man closer to God. To define goodness is an uphill task. We see it around us every day. Kind gestures of men and women who are not seeking any benefit. We see generosity without reason, calmness in crises, the willingness to risk one's wellbeing and life for the defense and the protection of others. We find these qualities of goodness in relatively non-descript people in the most unexpected of places and we get pleasantly surprised.

Goodness is something we can sense. I have seen it in poor people and sometimes amongst the affluent. You can sense goodness in the way people speak and behave. You can sense it in the old man who stands back when others push or the lady who is effusive in her gratitude for something you did as part of your job. Some part of us identifies with this goodness and for a certain limited period we act as if we too were good.

Another variety of goodness is one that identifies with a religion or a practice. You have good soldiers who conform to the rules and requirements of the organization, good Christians who attend church regularly and good people of other faiths. Goodness is measured here as concordance to custom or practice. Conformational goodness and core goodness are different entities although they may occasionally coexist.

A precept that religions and organizations often profess is that concordance with their faith or practice is essential to be considered good. Someone with might have core goodness, but his lack of confirmation makes him bad. This is an illogical and presumptuous assertion. God and heaven cannot be reached by diligent custom. Actions rather than affirmation are the key to the kingdom. Goodness and kindness are beyond religion and creed. They are the essence of humanity. Goodness begets goodness just as a smile evokes another in response. The balance between good and evil is what keeps the world sane. Let us appreciate good men, irrespective of their faith and if possible, emulate their cult, the cult of goodness.

The Evolution of Character

It is axiomatic to state that good and evil coexist in every individual. Similar external stimuli however, elicit discordant responses in different people. The responses to stimuli are influenced by a man's cultural background and tempered with age. Children's characters are the easiest to mould. Molding is better achieved by a nurturing environment rather than by didactic discourse.

The young are in a constant state of learning. They easily imbibe the actions and projected values of icons they wish to emulate. Parents, caretakers and teachers are the first people a child looks up to for example. The degree to which one emulates an elder is also proportional to the presumed indices of his success. It is appropriate therefore to highlight the presumed successes of desirable role models rather than to harp on their weaknesses for the benefit of the young. Life is long enough for the young to learn of evil and failure and to cultivate defenses against them.

Character is not, as often perceived irrevocably etched in a child's cerebral circuits. Our brain cells and their connections are in a constant state of rewiring. New connections are constantly being established while older ones are broken down. Contrary to earlier beliefs, it now known that nerve cell regeneration is an ongoing phenomenon throughout life. Over a period of time a monster can become humane and a saint satanic.

Bad habits are difficult to break and the evil often revert back to their original ways. This occurs due to the complexity of factors that control our actions. Lives experiences are stored in our memory templates. New learning and understanding creates newer connections which modulate the older ones. The strength, amplitude and frequency of reinforcement of positive experiences result in the subjugation of older negative traits or vice versa.

There are of course some pathological or injured minds which cannot be influenced. These are those who require pharmacological modulation or the now abandoned practices of electric shock or insulin coma therapies.

The Seasons of the Mind

There is a rhythm in every phenomenon of nature. The climate varies with the tilt of the earth's axis. The tides rise and fall with the pull of the sun and the moon. There are seasonal migrations and mating periods in the animal world.

The human internal milieu is equally subject to rhythms. The woman's reproductive cycles are the monthly cycles of ovulation and menstruation. Day-night and sleep-wake rhythms are influenced by melatonin. Are there inbuilt cycles of learning and physical activity? If there are cycles for intellectual and physical activity are they pre-programmed or do they occur like the cycles of hunger and satiety, stimulated by a biochemical trigger. It is rational to believe that there are phases of creativity which auger excellence in any field. As to whether these phases are under volitional control or are modulated by external influences remains conjunctural.

The Truth and Potency of Grand Mother's Cures

If you get drenched in the rain, you will catch a cold. This is Grand Mother's wisdom. It is true however that the scientific rationale behind many of these accurate assertions remains ambiguous. Acquiring a respiratory infection in a crowded environment is based on the simple laws of contagion and infection. Coryza or cold resulting from exposure is more difficult to explain We are warm blooded animals. A wet scalp or a chilly drizzle will not cause any significant change in our core temperatures. A constriction of blood vessels in response to cold is more likely to occur in the skin. A local immune failure in the throat in response to cold resulting in a proliferation of viral contagion is an unconvincing hypothesis. Yet we know for a fact that Granma is right.

The concept of hot and cold foods and the way in which these foods affect our constitution and even our behaviour are poorly explained by their caloric and protein contents. Why should bananas worsen a cold or cucumbers help you cool down in hot weather. Do cucumbers scavenge free radicals while bananas don't? One can stretch the truth with elaborate explanations. Few of these explanations would stand up to scientific scrutiny backed by what is described as class 1 evidence.

We have to accept with humility that grandma's dogmas and country wisdom have saved more lives and achieved more cures than many of the marvels of modern medicine.

The Virtue of Charity

There has been endless debate on whether there is virtue in charity. Should one give alms to beggars or a free meal to a starving man? There might be some truth in the assertion that charity perpetuates penury. The receiver gets used to free hand outs and does not want to work for his living any more. It is also accurate that in many metropolises begging is controlled by goons as an organized racket and the fruits of your charity do not stay with the beggar. This is part but not all of the truth.

The very sincerity of most beggars' pleas defy the supposition that your alms do not matter to him. Contrary to dramatic assertions by many, there are few beggars who change into their suits and drive off in their cars at the end of a day's begging. The occasional fraudster may pull this stunt, but you are more likely to get conned at a club or a place of worship by a swank confidence trickster.

Charity to someone poorer than you need not be rationalized. The bottled-up anxiety on unspent money is probably more dangerous than the perils of poverty. So, if you have a little loose change in your pocket hand it over to the nearest urchin and make a bee line for it before he alerts the others that there is a sucker around.

The Angst of Ishq and the Lacunae of Lakshya

It sounds discordant to discuss Ishq and Lakshya in the same essay. Both are strong terms and mean a good deal more than their English translations. An irrational pursuance of either can be detrimental. The emotions behind Ishq and Lakshya however are essential catalysts in the evolution of civilization. Ishq makes the world go round. Ishq has influenced world history more and resulted in the spilling of more innocent blood than avarice. It has spawned poetry, provoked beautiful paintings and spurred mankind in general to greater achievement.

Lakshya is more than focus. It is the clarity of vision in a sea of possibilities. It implies single mindedness of pursuit rather than ambition. Both Ishq and Lakshya imply a powerful emotional driving impetus. Either of them can be the impetus behind achievement or the spark behind conflagration.

Neither Ishq nor Lakshya are essential for existence. There can be love and happy marriages without Ishq. Ishq implies passion as well as love, possessiveness that transcends lust. Ishq consumes rather than comforts its victims. The warmth and comfort of long and fruitful relationships is beyond the passion of Ishq.

Lakshya is a powerful driving force that can consume the afflicted in the pursuance of a goal. Successful careers and rewarding professions are possible without the passion of Lakshya. A more rational and balanced approach to life has the innate advantage of a higher flexibility. Effort without the emotional overlay of lakshya provides for a more balanced life and a better adjusted personality.

Ishq and lakshya provide the twist of spice to mundane existence. They are exciting and not essential ingredients of civilization's ethos. We can survive without them, but they add life to living and excitement to existence.

Akbar the Mughal emperor encouraged intellectual debate. One of the questions he threw to his court was on the relative intensities of different types of love. After some debate, the wise men averred that the strongest love was the love a mother had for her babies. Birbal disagreed. The most consuming love was the love of one's own life. The other courtiers mocked him. Birbal agreed to put up a small demonstration. A female monkey with two babies was captured from Akbar's Garden. They were put into a shallow empty well with steep walls. There was a tree branch over the well which a full-grown monkey could jump and catch to escape. The babies would not be able to make it. The mother stayed on in the well with her young. The courtiers smiled. Birbal was proving their point. Attendants started filling up the well with water. The mother monkey jumped out. Seeing her babies in the well, she jumped back in and placed them on her shoulders. The courtiers applauded. Their point had been proven. Birbal raised his hands pleading for silence. The water level reached the monkeys chest. Suddenly shaking her babes from off her shoulders she jumped to safety. Birbal had made his point. The instinct for self-preservation is stronger than any maternal instinct. We are not sure as to whether the baby monkeys in the story were rescued. There was no SPCA to hound Birbal those days.

It is a point for debate, whether humans, with their higher degree of conditioned behavior would behave in the same manner as Birbal's monkeys. It is rational to think that they would. Instincts are architectonically senior to emotions. When it comes to a crunch, they take precedence over more evolved behavior patterns.

There are many examples of primordial behaviors that we come across daily. Some may be more dramatic, like stranded air crash victims engaging in cannibalism. Many criminal acts like rape and murder would also come under this category. Women leaving secure marriages for unsuitable relationships and young girls eloping with inappropriate men are also examples of instinct subordinating intelligence.

Modulation of instincts can be achieved through training. A soldier charging into battle for the flag is a dramatic illustration of a instinct subjugation. We come across civilians, putting themselves in peril to save others' lives. Courage is an evolved characteristic. A predator does not have courage. He attacks based on an instinctual realization of his superior strength over that of his prey. Courage defies odds. It attests to man's ascent over instinct. The survival of a civilized society depends on man curbing his instincts of greed and avarice in favor of magnanimity and generosity. Value systems are not ensconced didactically but by suitable example. It is imperative that the powerful and the influential, whether they be teachers or icons, ensure that the examples they set and the messages they impart are impeccably appropriate.

Shades Of Grey

Khalil Issac Mathai Palathinkal

They tell me, I should conform

Believe big brother on what is right and what is wrong

I look around and find no black or white

Only blurred and indistinct shades of grey

Laws and regulations are to protect the meek, not to curtail the strong

Don't curb desires, chide me about social norms

I breathe at my pace; I will step on no toes

Let me dance to my own rhythm, beat away my woes

What is right and what is wrong?

A terrorist is a man of God gone wrong

He believes in what he does with all his heart

Unlike a politician who fosters hate to garner votes

Moral policing, endless high ground posturing

You can live your life, just leave me alone

Spirits roaming free through the forest of life

To confirm mindlessly is to die

Why bust a rave party or beat a bar going girl

If coke is hazardous, ban it- not port

Tolerance comes from fulfillment, shift your focus within

To curb creativity is a deadly sin

It is the right of youth to roam free

Life after all is a journey of self-discovery

We all have to search and find our own paths

To lives destination- let us follow our hearts

Moral Policing   Khalil Issac Mathai Palathinkal

*T*he women in red were beaten blue

Clothes torn, dignity in shreds, in the camera's glare

Hindu hooligans, the Taliban, brothers of a clan

Hate brewed in discontent, robots in a diabolical plan

Can youth's energies be channeled else where

Or is rhetoric a balm on unfilled chores

Young people, sickened, wasting their lives

Puppeteered by charlatans, society pays the price

The cost of sustaining these misguided souls

Running amok though the fabric of society, so delicately woven

Crimson streaks on delicate embroidery

Scars unhealing, in the fabric of life

The hazards of moral policing, the hypocrisy of intolerance

Religious resurgence for rationalization of imcompetence

Whipping frantic followers into a frenzy of self-deception

Red eyes see red, a jaundiced view point

The euphoric flagellation of cacophonic clichés

False promise to the herd by pied pipers in politics

The creation of issues, dramatic and theotrical

Gluttonous ravaging wolves in nationalistic garb

Preying on the masses with charismatic appeal

Big brother breathing down your neck spews vitriol

'I am the law, the conscience of the ages

What I say is wisdom distilled from the sages'

Say the guardian of a nebulous heritage

****

Flavors Of Life

Khalil Issac Mathai Palathinkal

I have been though it

The shock as my friend lost control, one should not drink and drive

I forgive him, it was an error of immaturity

A belief in one's immortality or ignorance of vulnerability

He survived with scratches, my neck snapped

The bike was wreck

I felt no pain- but my body wouldn't move

My breathing was laboured, I could barely speak

The doctors chattering around put a collar on me

I heard mumbles of sympathy, poor chap, they said- he is finished

There was an operation, my neck bones were fixed

I hoped I could walk again – it was not to be

There were odd sensations in my legs- that was all

A severed spinal cord's aphaptic impulses, not useful

False promises from quacks, vague newspaper claims

Of stem cell and supplements, shortcuts to fame

My body was mine, just not in my control

There were skin sores, urine infections and muscle spasms

Belief in quick fire fixes faded, but hope did not

I was alive and my mind was sharp and agile

Sympathy is demeaning; inspiration nurtures the fire of my being

A mind liberated, I would achieve much more

The pain of loss is numbed by the promise of struggle

In my mind I fly, while you walk

Desires soar and achievements mean so much more

I am cushioned by love and nurtured by care

The days ahead blossom with hope, not despair

Questions remain, will a miracle make me stand again

Can I father a child, cal I love and be loved

     I learn to take each day as it comes- sips of joy and some sorrow,

…………………………………………………………….